Chloe opened the door to her rental that was parked two empty spaces over from Tristan's.

His hat sat on the front passenger seat. She reached over and picked it up, and when she stood straight, she glanced over her shoulder.

Tristan was walking toward her.

Her heart sped up as the last of the cars drove away.

They were alone.

As he stood in front of Chloe, he gave her one of his small, sexy smiles. "Is that for me, Ace?"

His gaze dropped to the ball cap clutched in her hand then rose back up to her eyes.

Give him the hat and endure two more weeks of wanting his kisses and dreaming about his caresses. Or be with him in every way that she desired for the short time they had left. Those were her options.

Chloe took his Stetson off his head and put it on hers. Then she kissed him.

* * *

TILLBRIDGE STABLES:
These ranchers are roping horses—and hearts!

Dear Reader,

Thank you for choosing *The Cowboy's Claim* as your new romance read.

I never dreamed that I would write a book about a cowboy and an actress meeting at a horse boarding stable in Maryland. It came about when I shared with a few people that I had a collection of bull-rider trading cards. Several conversations later over glasses of wine, Chloe Daniels and Tristan Tillbridge falling in love at his family-owned business, Tillbridge Horse Stable & Guesthouse, bloomed into this story.

Tristan was cut out of his father's will and is working hard to get back what should have been his inheritance. It's an uphill battle. The last thing he wants cluttering up his schedule is "babysitting" a pampered actress...especially since she's scared of horses. Chloe may be afraid of horses, but she's not afraid of hard work or standing up to the sexy former bull rider. Writing about these two finding their way to each other made me laugh, cry and smile.

Like many of us, Tristan and Chloe are both striving toward what is important to them. Ambition will take them in opposite directions. But as the saying goes, "the heart wants what the heart wants." Sometimes allowing our hearts to take the lead can bring us to wonderful people and places. Do you agree?

I'd love to hear from you. Visit www.ninacrespo.com and say hello. While you're there, sign up for my newsletter and follow me on social media. Instagram and Facebook are two of my favorite places to share information about my books and upcoming appearances. I look forward to seeing you there.

Nina

The Cowboy's Claim

NINA CRESPO

HARLEQUIN
SPECIAL
EDITION

HARLEQUIN®
SPECIAL EDITION™

Recycling programs for this product may not exist in your area.

ISBN-13: 978-1-335-89463-2

The Cowboy's Claim

Copyright © 2020 by Nina Crespo

All rights reserved. No part of this book may be used or reproduced in any manner whatsoever without written permission except in the case of brief quotations embodied in critical articles and reviews.

This is a work of fiction. Names, characters, places and incidents are either the product of the author's imagination or are used fictitiously. Any resemblance to actual persons, living or dead, businesses, companies, events or locales is entirely coincidental.

This edition published by arrangement with Harlequin Books S.A.

For questions and comments about the quality of this book, please contact us at CustomerService@Harlequin.com.

Harlequin Enterprises ULC
22 Adelaide St. West, 40th Floor
Toronto, Ontario M5H 4E3, Canada
www.Harlequin.com

Printed in U.S.A.

Nina Crespo lives in Florida, where she indulges in her favorite passions—the beach, a good glass of wine, date night with her own real-life hero and dancing. Her lifelong addiction to romance began in her teens while on a "borrowing spree" in her older sister's bedroom, where she discovered her first romance novel. Let Nina's sensual contemporary stories feed your own addiction for love, romance and happily-ever-after. Visit her at ninacrespo.com.

Books by Nina Crespo

Harlequin Special Edition

Tillbridge Stables

The Cowboy's Claim

Visit the Author Profile page at Harlequin.com for more titles.

Chapter One

It was perfect riding weather at Tillbridge Horse Stable. All Tristan Tillbridge needed was a horse and some time to enjoy the morning. He had plenty of horses, but based on the number of what-the-hells ganging up for his attention, enjoyment wasn't on his schedule anytime soon.

He dropped his black-booted foot from the bottom rail of the white ladder fence circling the small arena where a blond horse trainer exercised Moonlight Joy, a golden creamy-maned palomino. "So you were driving the back road last night and found the south pasture gate wide-open?"

"Yeah." Mace Calderone stood beside him. His brown deputy's hat cast a shadow over his bronze face. "The winds from the rainstorm could have caused it."

"Or someone left it that way." Tristan stripped off his tan Rough Rider work gloves, flipped up the shirttail of his navy pullover and stuffed the gloves in his back jeans pocket. "The staff knows the 'close every gate' rule, but everyone else can't read a damn sign. Since the guesthouse and cottages opened on the property six months ago, stopping them from breaking, trampling or opening things they shouldn't is becoming a full-time job."

Next to the one he already had as stable manager.

"I hear you. These days it seems like rules are considered more of a suggestion than a requirement." Mace glanced over his shoulder. "Looks like you got a stray."

On the wide dirt and gravel path leading from the stable farther behind them, a woman with long dark curly hair wearing oversize aviator sunglasses talked animatedly on her cell.

As she threw up her hand in frustration over something the person on the line told her, the front of her cropped yellow blazer opened wider revealing a snowy-white, fitted top. Matching skinny jeans molded to her long legs. Each step forward brought her and her red high-heeled boots—designer, no doubt—closer to fresh horse shit.

Mace turned to watch. "Five bucks she saves the shoes."

"Ten, she doesn't."

She swerved right and Mace grinned. "Instead of cash, you can pay me with a beer this weekend."

"That's fine, but I won't be the one buying."

The woman veered left, still talking on her phone and digging into her large red purse.

Mace's smile disappeared. "She really isn't paying attention."

"Told you." But not even the sure win of a bet could let Tristan stand by and watch what would probably be the worst part of her day unfold.

He and Mace called out at the same time. "Hey! Look out!"

But too absorbed in her conversation, she traipsed ahead...right into the steaming fresh pile. As she skidded forward, the phone flew out of her hand and after a few long breath-holding seconds of teetering on her heels, she finally caught her balance.

Mace winced. "That could have been ugly. I'll make sure she's okay. Unless you're interested. She's cute."

Sunglasses pushed up on her head, the woman bent down and retrieved her cell. As she stood straight, she alternated between shaking the dirtied boot on her foot and glancing at the bottom of it with a grossed-out expression.

Interested in a woman who wore high heels to a stable, and from a distance, faintly resembled his deceased father's spoiled, devious second wife? Yeah, he'd pass. "I have a meeting in a few minutes. She's all yours."

The two-way radio clipped to Mace's tactical belt crackled to life. *"Calling all units in the southeast. Multiple reports of traffic backing up on Colton Road at the interstate exit. Motorists need assistance."*

He clicked a button on his shoulder mic. "Dispatch.

Unit seven in route." Mace looked to Tristan. "You'll have to help her out."

"I'm not the one wearing the badge. Rescuing people is your job."

"I would, but duty calls. You can tell me her name later." Mace clapped him on the back, then strode to his patrol car parked in the grass on the other side of the ring.

Tristan headed to the woman. Why couldn't people just obey the multiple signs on the paved trail from the guesthouse that stated: No visitors allowed at the stable until 10:00 a.m. on Mondays.

"I can't believe this." The woman glanced up at Tristan while gingerly scraping the sole of her boot on the ground. "Is this stuff literally everywhere— even in the main areas?"

Yards behind her, two grooms wearing blue short-sleeved pullovers and jeans rode horses with black manes and mahogany coats at a steady trot.

"Move out of the way." Tristan picked up the pace and closed the distance.

"You don't have to ye—" She did a double take at the oncoming horses and froze. Annoyance quickly faded from her eyes along with the color from her smooth brown cheeks.

He grabbed hold of her arm and ushered her to the side of the path. As the bays went past, she turned toward him and squeezed her eyes shut.

Her barely detectable tremors vibrated into him. Was she afraid of the horses? On a reflex, he lightly grasped her arms and put himself between her and the bays. The sweet lemon fragrance wafting from her skin was like a welcome cool breeze. It roused memories of lazy summer afternoons, lying in his hammock in the shade with a cold drink in his hand, lost in the perfection of nothing on his mind. He hadn't enjoyed an afternoon like that in a long time.

"Thanks." Her soft exhale rushed over his throat spreading goose bumps over him. She tilted up her head and her long lashes rose.

His heart tripped. Mace had gotten it only partially right. She was more than just cute.

Caught between wanting to gently sweep back the curls partially concealing her deep coppery eyes and staring at her lush full lips that were meant for long, slow, kisses, he remained suspended in the moment. Her loosening her death grip from his forearm prompted him to let her go.

The pop song ringtone blaring from her cell snapped his priorities back in place.

It didn't matter that she was pretty and smelled like his all-time favorite flavor. She didn't belong there if she was afraid of horses. Had she startled one of the bays, she or the riders could have been hurt. If she wanted to play Monday morning phone tag, she needed to do it someplace else.

Just as she went to answer her cell phone he intervened. "This isn't the place for you to talk on your phone. You have to stay alert, especially around the horses. In fact, you shouldn't be here." Tristan pointed to the paved trail intersecting the path. "Like the signs back there said, guests aren't allowed at the stable at this time of the morning."

"I am alert." A healthy glow returned to her face. "And I'm exactly where I should be. I'm meeting the person in charge of the stable at nine o'clock."

"About?"

"That's between me and them."

"I'm the stable manager, and you're not on my schedule."

"That's because *we're* not meeting." She gave him a "take that" smile.

Stubborn and a belief that rules didn't apply to her. Maybe she actually *was* a version of his father's second wife.

She was obviously in the wrong place. It was time to hand her over to the one person who could clear up exactly where she belonged. His cousin, Zurie. But one thing was certain. She wasn't on Zurie's schedule either. He was meeting with her that morning to talk about his expansion plan for the stable and to touch base about their staff appreciation get-together that was happening in a few weeks. She was squeezing the time in to talk with him before she headed to the airport to fly to Nevada for a conference.

Just as he went to call Zurie, he spotted his petite cousin farther up the path walking briskly toward them. Her straight black hair, gathered in a ponytail, swung behind her. She was dressed similarly to him in jeans and black work boots, but she wore a crisp blue Tillbridge Stable logoed button-down instead.

He looked to the woman. "Sure you don't want to change your story about why you're here?"

"No. I don't."

He almost felt sorry for her. Zurie had less patience for rule breakers and trespassers than he did. "It's your head."

She slid the strap of her bag higher on her shoulder. "My head is staying right where it belongs."

Chapter Two

Chloe sent her agent, Lena, a brief text apologizing for the sudden hang up, and not answering her call back. As she dropped her phone in her purse, she met the guy's direct stare.

With his close-cut dark hair, compelling hazel-brown eyes, and the near perfect angles of his light brown face, he had *GQ* potential written all over him, even with his irritated expression.

He crossed his arms over his chest, and muscles formed underneath the stable's logo—a white horse and *T* with a lasso around it—embroidered on the left side of his shirt.

A minute ago, she'd been tempted to soothe her embarrassment over almost planting her butt in the dirt by snuggling closer to all of that tall, hot-man goodness.

Until he'd accused her of trespassing. He thought she was ruining his day? If he only knew about the crap she'd been dealing with before literally stepping in it.

Her morning had actually started out great. She'd had an early breakfast with two actors in DC who were going to use her one-bedroom apartment just outside of Los Angeles as an Airbnb for a month while she was in Maryland.

Their enthusiasm for acting along with their encouragement about her own career had reignited her optimism that had started to wane because of a few bad breaks. But once she'd left them, her morning had gone downhill fast.

The two-hour drive to just outside of the town of Bolan had taken longer than anticipated. After several wrong turns, due to the not so helpful map app on her phone, she'd finally figured out where to go and pulled into the parking lot of Tillbridge Horse Stable and Guesthouse. Then, her agent, Lena, had called with news. It had thrown her so completely, she'd forgotten to change out of her favorite boots into more practical shoes before trekking to the stable.

Don't take it personally. The executives at Drippy Dry have decided to go a different way... That's what Lena had said when she'd informed her the company had fired her from their commercial campaign.

It had finally happened. At twenty-eight, her career had hit an all-time low. She couldn't even keep an acting part in a commercial selling glow-in-the-dark zombie-printed paper towels.

Gnawing defeat pierced through frustration and

plummeted deep inside of her. Almost nine months had passed since she'd won a substantial role or been contacted about a script, the equivalent of a decade for an actor. Sporadic walk-on television roles and commercials didn't pay as much as a part in a film or a steady television series. Some months, she struggled to pay the bills.

That's why she had to erase any doubts Holland Ainsley, currently the hottest movie producer and director on the planet, might have about choosing her for a role in her upcoming futuristic Western film. The original actress Holland and the other producers had chosen had bowed out. They were actively searching for someone else, but issues with another film Holland was working on demanded her attention, and she refused to be distracted from it so auditions had been delayed. The good news was, it gave Chloe more time to prepare.

Lena sending her to a place in "Small Town, Maryland" to research life at a horse stable was a plot twist for her. She'd expected her to suggest spending time at a ranch or a horse farm in the Southwest, but if shadowing the manager of the stable for the next six weeks would help her to get that part—no, *the* part that would jump-start her career—nothing, including Mr. Grumpy-But-Hot, would stop her. She'd soak up everything about Tillbridge, the landscape, the people... even the horses.

As she glanced at the horses she'd encountered on the path, now in the arena, a smaller version of the anxiety that had gripped her earlier expanded inside of her chest. She was eleven the last time she'd been around a horse. They were just as big as she remembered them to be when she'd made the mistake of trying to ride one.

When the spooked horse had bolted down the trail that morning at summer camp, years ago, she'd gone from a brave, boasting volunteer to a frightened mess, and broken her arm.

A ghost of the remembered pain sent tingles through her right elbow.

People will feel sorry for you now because you got hurt, but all they'll remember in the future is how you fell off. That's why you have to learn everything there is to know first about whatever you plan to do before joining in. And make sure you're the best at it or don't do it at all.

That had been her father's take on the situation when she'd gotten home. That advice, as harsh as it had been, had kept her out of trouble. She'd never shown up unprepared for anything, big or small, but this time, "just fake it" would have to become her new motto. At least she wasn't expected to actually get on a horse for her audition. From what Lena had said, the role in the film may not even require getting on one at all. She just needed to learn about stable life and become comfortable with it…or at least act like she was.

The woman walking down the path joined them. An inner radiance lit up the delicate features of her dark brown face. "Hi. I'm Zurie Tillbridge. You must be Chloe Daniels."

"Yes." Chloe returned Zurie's firm handshake and smile. "Thank you for letting me stay here."

"Lena said it was important. I'm happy to help. I see you met my cousin Tristan."

Tristan. So that was his name. She'd met him if snapping at her was considered an introduction. "Yes, we've met."

A hint of irritation came into his neutral expression. "You scheduled another meeting here this morning?"

"I did." The smile on Zurie's face dimmed from friendly to professional.

Chloe's family drama radar locked in. *Ooh...interesting.* Zurie was clearly in charge, and he respected her, but something other than who was the bigger boss divided them. Jealousy? An inheritance dispute? Had one of them been a secret baby? Whatever the issue was, observing their relationship could lead to a gold mine of information for developing the character she wanted to play.

Tristan gave a curt nod and broke the silence. "I'll leave you to it. Find me when you're ready for us to meet."

He turned to walk away, but Zurie put a hand on his forearm. "Not so fast. We'll meet about the expansion when I get back. Her visit is what I wanted to talk about. Chloe's an actress, and she's here to research a part for a film. I'd planned on showing her around but my schedule has changed. I'm going to Florida instead of Nevada. A colleague who's a visiting faculty member for an equine studies program has to take time off because of a family emergency. I agreed to fill in for her. I'll be gone for six to eight weeks instead of a couple of days."

"But I'm supposed to shadow you for the next six weeks," Chloe objected.

"Tristan will have to take over for me."

He shook his head. "My schedule is full. I don't have time to babysit anyone."

Seriously? He thought she needed a babysitter? Not now or ever. Chloe faced him and flashed an overly sweet smile. "Oh, don't worry about me. I'm fine on my own."

"You're afraid of horses and that's a problem, especially if you're hanging around my stable."

"The problem was that I just didn't expect to *see* one." She followed his gaze to her soiled boot and heat bloomed in her cheeks. "What I meant to say is the horses caught me off guard."

His brow raised. "So that's what you're sticking with? You were caught off guard to see horses at a horse stable?"

"Hold on." Zurie put up her hand. "I don't know what happened between the two of you before I got here, but I have a plane to catch." She looked to Chloe. "If you want to observe operations at Tillbridge, you're going to have to shadow the person stepping into my shoes." She looked to Tristan. "Whoever is in charge of Tillbridge during the time I'm away will be the one to show Ms. Daniels the ropes. If you don't think you can handle both of those duties, I'll assign someone who can."

Chapter Three

Tristan drove the golf cart down the narrow paved trail winding through the green landscape, and the wheels dipped in and out of every separation in the pavement.

Chloe sat on the passenger side, digging her fingers into the cushion underneath her as she bounced in the seat.

They rounded a curve and zipped by a fenced-in pasture with horses on one side, and on the other, a worker riding a large mower in the empty field.

The scents of rich earth and freshly cut grass intertwined with the smell of horse manure. Yeah, it was everywhere. Chloe couldn't stop a grimace as she glanced at her dirty boot. She'd have to get used to dealing with it along with Tristan.

He hadn't spoken or looked at her since having a

side conversation with Zurie at the stable. She couldn't hear what they'd discussed, but from their hard expressions and the stiffness of their body language when they'd gone their separate ways, it hadn't gone well. She'd told him she could walk back to the guesthouse, but he'd insisted on giving her a ride. Probably to keep her from wandering around *his* stable.

At the end of the path, he steered into the parking lot on the side of the green-roofed two-story white building with green trim and a pitched roof. Sunglasses hid his eyes. "Car?"

"There." Chloe pointed to the red two-door midway down the first row.

Based on his current mood, she actually preferred his choice of not talking to her at all or communicating in monosyllabic caveman-speak.

He pulled up behind the rental and hit the brake.

As she lurched forward, she banged the toe of her boot. Chloe started counting to ten and made it to four. "Why are you so mad about me being here?"

"Do you honestly want to know?"

"Yes."

He removed his sunglasses and the force of his gaze pinned her to the seat. "First, my schedule is already packed without adding more to it. Second, the stable is busy in general so it's not the best time to have someone tagging along, and third, what we do here isn't acting. We work hard. The only way you can learn about this place is actually digging in and sweating through the day-to-day, not rolling over the surface and acting the part for entertainment."

"Hold on a minute. I know how to work hard, and yes, acting is about entertainment, but that doesn't mean that the role I'm auditioning for isn't important for people to see."

"What part is it?"

A based-on-real-life scientist who studied the effects of climate changes on animals in an effort to save them from extinction. She actually had tried out for that part a few weeks ago, but just like with the Drippy Dry commercial, she hadn't gotten that one either.

If she told him that was the part she was auditioning for now, he might see her in a different light—but lying would mean she felt the need to justify herself and her choice of roles. She didn't. Using her imagination to create enjoyment for people by transporting them into a different world was nothing to be ashamed of.

Chloe looked directly into his eyes. "The friend of a supernatural horse whisperer who owns a horse farm."

He put his sunglasses back on and muttered. "That figures."

A held-back suggestion of where to put his "that figures" almost set her mouth on fire, but she had better things to do than argue. She got out of the golf cart. "When and where should I meet you?"

"Philippa Gale is the manager and chef for the guesthouse. You're meeting her here at ten o'clock."

"I'm supposed to be shadowing you."

"I have to sort out my schedule first. I'll get back to you. I've got people waiting for me. There's a new horse coming in, and I'm late. I have to go." Tristan released the brake on the golf cart and sped off.

Sort out his schedule? She wasn't going to just sit on her butt waiting around for him to decide when he'd get back to her. Like she'd told him earlier, she was fine on her own.

She hauled her purple suitcase and carry-on bag out of the trunk of her car, then wheeled them up the side ramp to the covered white-pillared porch.

A soft breeze swayed green rocking chairs in front of windows framed by green shutters. In the distance, at the bottom of a gently sloping grassy incline, horses grazed in a fenced-in pasture.

Seconds passed before she registered why she'd paused and drawn in such a deep breath. The clean, fresh air was devoid of exhaust fumes. And the view was stunning.

She walked through the double-door entry into a dark, wood-floored modern space boasting just enough country living accents. Gold framed paintings of horses running and grazing in rolling fields and near mountains hung on white walls.

Chloe continued straight ahead past a seating area with two navy couches surrounding a stained natural wood coffee table to the reception counter.

The slim brunette standing behind it wearing a navy blouse with the stable's logo smiled. "Hello. Welcome to Tillbridge."

The woman checked Chloe in and gave her a key card. On a map featuring the twenty-room guesthouse, she pointed out the adjoining Pasture Lane Restaurant along with the guest cottages on the property, the stable and the general area.

Chloe folded the map and stuck it in her purse. "Can you tell me where I can find Philippa Gale? I'm supposed to meet her in a half hour."

"Try the restaurant. One of the staff will be able to tell you where she is."

"Thank you."

Upstairs in her room, Chloe stripped off her red boots in the mahogany-floored entryway and left them by the door.

The smell from her boot diminished in the light scent of pine polish used on the wood furniture in the room.

She put her purse and carry-on bag on top of the dresser to her left. Then she placed her suitcase on the padded bench to the right that was sitting at the foot of the queen-size bed with a blue quilted headboard and covered with a sumptuous cream comforter. Another beautiful view pulled her to the side window.

A green lawn extended from the side of the guesthouse to the tree line where the beginning of a paved trail was visible. Where did it lead? To a pasture or another scenic spot? She'd have to explore where later.

Holland believed the outdoors stimulated creativity. In fact, she had sent the actors for the snowbound blizzard drama she'd directed to live in the wilds of Alaska for a month so they could acclimate to how the area could affect the characters they'd played. The snowmageddon film, as it was often called, had received multiple accolades, and the lead actress had won an award for her performance.

Sure, the part she was auditioning for wasn't the

lead, but if she was great, which she would be, it would move her from mediocracy to prominence as an actress. And possibly open the door to an even larger future—becoming a director and someday a producer.

When it came to women she admired who were working behind the camera, Holland Ainsley was her shero. The films she directed were gracefully unfolding stories that featured breathtaking visuals, and unflinching performances that were thought-provoking. Holland was also known for not being afraid to fight for her vision or for more opportunities for women to direct and produce in Hollywood.

If she made Holland aware of her interest, Holland might consider talking with her and provide guidance of how she could move ahead.

But none of that would happen if she didn't get over her apprehension around horses and nail winning the part.

Earlier, she really had just been caught off guard to see them that up close and personal so soon after arriving. Well, she'd actually been closer to Tristan than the horses. The light clean scent, which wasn't cologne, that had emanated from him had been so soothing. It had reminded her of a cooling summer rain and taken her mind off the horses, but how good he'd smelled wasn't the point. She hadn't been prepared for the experience of seeing what had once caused her worst nightmare. Next time, she would be.

She wasn't a frightened child trapped on the back of a large runaway creature. She was an adult consciously grabbing hold of her future. This was about taking the necessary steps, even baby ones—like not freezing up again when she saw a horse. She could do this.

Chloe drew in a deep inhale, then released it along with her doubt and lingering childhood memories. She opened her suitcase on the bench. After changing into a white blouse and blue jeans, she unpacked the boots she'd splurged on before she'd left for Maryland.

The smooth glossy black knee-high riding boots were fashionable and eye-catching, but also said "I know what I'm doing, look at me." Definitely not appropriate. Chloe picked up the second pair—brown vintage-looking cowboy boots. They had such an easy-breezy fun vibe. She traced over the distressed leather and excitement buzzed at the thought of slipping them on.

But as much as she loved them, they didn't support the attitude she wanted to convey while observing the staff. Despite what Tristan believed, she wasn't there for attention nor was she expecting the "star treatment."

Setting them aside, she dug a little deeper in her bag and found her low-key black flat ankle boots with a tread sole. They were a better choice and wouldn't cause her to stand out for the wrong reason.

Ten minutes ahead of her meeting, she walked downstairs to the Pasture Lane Restaurant.

Natural light from a wall of glass and tall green potted plants gave the pale wood-floored space an open, airy feel. Casually dressed patrons occupied half of the two dozen or so wood tables accented by green padded chairs.

Chloe seated herself as the sign on the hostess stand indicated, choosing a corner table near a window.

A blonde college-aged woman rushed around delivering food and taking orders. Her shirt said I NEED COFFEE… MY HORSE… AND A NAP, but from the look on her pink flushed face, she could also use another server waiting tables.

Been there. Working shorthanded was the worst.

When she'd moved from Cincinnati to Los Angeles, shortly after her college graduation seven years ago, she'd waited tables to pay the bills in between auditions.

Those early days of her acting career had been tough but rewarding. Not only had she waited tables, but she'd also worked as a receptionist at Television City. That had led to her snagging an assistant's position that had opened the door to meeting more people in the industry, including Lena.

It had taken three years for her to get her first real break—a temporary role on a soap opera. After that, she'd landed minor parts including one in a cable television series. It had ended after one season, but good reviews on her acting had provided enough street cred for her to get hired for small parts in film and television, and later, her last role, a reoccurring character in a cable crime drama series. She'd just been promoted to series regular when the network decided to take the show off the air. It had been a tough reminder of just how easily opportunities could disappear and to never take them for granted.

The young woman stopped at Chloe's table carrying a white thermal carafe. "Good morning, my name is Bethany. I'll be your server today. Would you like some coffee?"

"Yes, please."

Chloe smiled her thanks as Bethany filled her cup. "I'm here to see Philippa Gale? I have an appointment."

"Chef Gale is busy in the kitchen, but I'll let her know you're here. May I have your name?"

"Chloe Daniels."

Bethany stopped to clear a nearby table, then hurried through the double doors at the other end of the room.

A moment later, a tall woman around Chloe's age emerged from the kitchen.

The lime-green bandanna securing her dark locks matched her chef's coat and the Crocs visible under the hem of her black pants.

She strode over to the table. "Hello, Ms. Daniels." A faint lilt added a Southern flavor to her words. "I'm Philippa."

"Please, call me Chloe."

Philippa sat down. The smattering of freckles on her light brown face and her friendly smile gave her a youthful appearance, but an all-business mindset reflected in her brown eyes. "Tristan called earlier about you interviewing me today for your article."

"Article?" Apparently monosyllabic, caveman-speak didn't encompass enough words to explain the situation properly. "No, I'm not a writer. I'm an actress. I'm here for a few weeks to research a part."

A near eye roll came with Philippa's huff of exasperation. "Look. I hate to put you off, but the guesthouse is fully booked with an antiquing tour group, I'm short-staffed and we're prepping for the lunch rush."

Tristan knew the restaurant schedule and probably the staffing situation. Was he trying to set her up for failure or just drilling home his belief that everyone had something important to do at Tillbridge but her?

The only way you can learn about this place is actually digging in and sweating through the day-to-day, not rolling over the surface and acting out a part for entertainment...

Tristan's words ticked like pebbles on a window in Chloe's mind. "I can help."

"No. You're a guest."

"I have front and back of the house restaurant experience. I'll also learn a lot more through participation than just observation. Helping you helps me." Philippa's hesitation drove Chloe to her feet. "If I'm more of a nuisance than a help to you, I'll leave—no questions asked."

But Philippa kicking her out wouldn't happen. She wasn't going to screw up a chance to get better acquainted with the operation or prove Tristan wrong.

Philippa stared at Chloe as if working out an internal debate. She stood. "Come on then."

Chloe followed her. Just like when she stepped on set for the first time, jitters of excitement arose at the prospect of tackling something new.

Philippa would probably assign her more of the grunt work like wrapping the silverware in the napkins and setting up glassware and condiments in the server stations. She could also help by clearing tables and bringing out food. It had been a while since she'd done it, but she'd be okay once she got started.

In the kitchen, the scents of bacon and freshly baked bread just coming out of a double-tiered oven along the wall filled the medium-sized red-tiled space. Cooks stirred pots of food on the two gas burner stoves in the center island. Across the kitchen, another worker chopped salad vegetables at a stainless steel table.

Chloe's mouth watered. She'd definitely sample the food later.

She went with Philippa into a section off from the main area.

A pass-through dishwasher sat on one side of the space. On the other side, dirty pots and pans cluttered a three-compartment sink.

Philippa turned to her. "We've been staying on top of cleaning dishes, but as you can see, we're behind on the pots and pans. You'll want to get a jump on them before more dishes come in. I have plastic aprons in my office."

Like a new foreign language she had to translate, seconds passed before Chloe caught on to what Philippa meant. "You want me to scrub pots and wash dishes?"

"For now."

Chloe remained at a loss for words. Well, she *had* mentioned having back of the house experience. If she reneged on her offer now, she'd seem insincere, and undoubtedly, Tristan would hear what happened and gloat about it, one arrogantly spaced out word at a time.

"Okay then." Chloe resisted glancing at her recently manicured nails. "I should get started."

Chapter Four

The 4:45 a.m. alarm chimed on Chloe's cell.

Lying in bed, still more asleep than awake, she blindly reached out for her phone on the bedside table. After a couple tries, she found it, hit Snooze and clutched it to her chest. But it couldn't be morning already. She'd just fallen asleep.

Yesterday, after she'd helped out by washing dishes and pots for the breakfast and lunch service, two of the bussers had called in sick, leaving the restaurant seriously shorthanded for dinner. Understanding the consequences of that for the waitstaff firsthand, and seeing their downcast expressions as they anticipated the rough night ahead, her conscience wouldn't just let her order a meal to go and walk out. She'd stayed and pitched in as a busser clearing tables.

Afterward, she'd come back to her room, just after ten at night, with barely enough energy to brush her teeth and throw on an oversized sleep shirt before collapsing in bed. She'd even skipped her usual face cleansing routine, not that beauty mattered anymore. She'd said goodbye to her manicure after scrubbing the first dirty pot, given up on maintaining her makeup once the steam from the dishwasher had melted it off. And forget about flat ironing her hair when she got up in five minutes—make that ten—her curls were going into a ponytail. She'd agreed to help out in the kitchen again.

Chloe moved to put the phone back on the table but lifting her arm took too much effort. Her muscles ached from head to toe. What was that saying? *Sacrifice for the sake of art...* And it was already starting to pay off.

Yesterday, helping the restaurant through a jam had not only increased her standing with the kitchen and waitstaff, but the lodging staff, too. A few had gone out of their way to introduce themselves to her in the staff break room, and on her way back to her guest room last night, the front desk clerk had slipped her one of the special VIP welcome packages reserved for guests in the cottages. She'd definitely put the contents—a moisturizing bath bomb, a bottle of wine and a small box of chocolates, all from local merchants in the area—to good use when she returned to her room that afternoon or whenever she finished for the day.

If she played her cards right, she could get the staff to talk about the true inner workings of the place. Yesterday, she'd overheard snippets of a conversation between Philippa and the housekeeping supervisor about Zurie, Tristan and ownership in the stable. Something about him finally getting his share of Tillbridge back? She'd wanted to ask some of the staff about it, but it was too soon for anyone to feel comfortable giving her the tell-all on the Tillbridges, yet.

Adding the business dynamics to the tension she'd sensed earlier between Tristan and Zurie would bring even more to the character she was developing for her audition. And honestly, she was curious about Tristan. Was he always scowling and serious?

The Drake song she'd programmed for Lena's number chimed on her cell. Lena, who was just as anxious as she was about her winning a part in Holland's film, was probably checking in for an update on her progress.

Chloe answered. "Don't you sleep?"

"I will, after I talk to my favorite client. How are things with you?"

"Fine." Chloe rested the back of her hand over her closed eyes. "But I'd love to be in your shoes right now. Just going to bed sounds amazing. I could use some more sleep."

"You've only been there a day. Is Zurie's schedule that intense?"

"She isn't here. She was called away to teach at some university."

"Called away?" Lena's voice rose an octave, and what sounded like sheets rustled in the background. Knowing her, she'd gotten out of bed. "If she's not there, who's showing you around?"

"No one, but I've been busy. I helped out in the restaurant yesterday, and I'll probably be there for most of today."

"What? Why are you working in the restaurant?"

"Because they're shorthanded."

"I don't care what they are. I'm calling Zurie to straighten this out."

Chloe quickly sat up. "No. Don't. It's okay."

"It's not okay. You're not trying out for a role as a cook or a waitress. If they're that shorthanded in the restaurant, they need to hire people."

"They are."

"It sounds like you're being used."

Used. From Lena's point of view that was an ugly four-letter word. As a former child star, who'd been screwed over financially by her manager and her parents, Lena was tenacious when it came to protecting her clients. If she didn't pull Lena back now, Lena would move straight into fix-it mode.

"Relax, Lena. I'm not being taken advantage of. I volunteered."

"You what?" Lena's tone rose even higher than before.

Ugh! This was almost impossible to explain without an adequate dose of caffeine. "I know this is not what you had in mind for me when you set this up with Zurie, but I came here to really learn about life at a stable so I can genuinely act the part during my audition. The best way for me to learn the inner workings of this place is digging in and sweating through the day-to-day, not rolling over the surface." Wait. She did not just quote Tristan. She really did need a hit of caffeine if something he said was her go-to for a pass-able explanation.

Lena released a long breath and paused. "Fine. I'll hold off on calling Zurie, for now, but don't forget. This is an important audition for you. You're one of Holland's top picks, but the competition is fierce. Everyone and their mother is sniffing around this opportunity, but the one way you can set yourself apart is by impressing her with your knowledge of horse stables, so step it up on the sweating through the day-to-day part but with the horses."

"I will."

"You say that now, but I'm afraid without a nudge your little phobia might get in the way of your progress."

"It's not a phobia…exactly. More like a teeny discomfort around horses." That might possibly cause her to panic, freeze up or hyperventilate until she passed out from lack of oxygen whenever she was around them.

The doubt she'd managed yesterday started creeping back in. *No. You're consciously grabbing hold of the future. Remember?*

"I can't believe Zurie just left you like that and didn't assign someone to take her place," Lena said. "Is there someone else at the stable who can show you the ropes?

Tristan. She could tattle on him, but as much fun as it would be to sic Lena on Tristan, that phone call would only nose-dive her current chilly relationship with him to an Arctic level freeze.

And worse, letting someone else fight her battles

would just support his theory that she couldn't handle being there. He didn't seem to be in a hurry to help her out, but maybe she didn't really need him. The staff members she'd met so far were friendly. If she asked around, someone might be willing to assist her in learning what she needed to know. Especially if she continued to make herself useful.

"Lena, really, I have the situation under control."

"Are you sure? You can't afford any distractions, because if you bomb during this audition—"

"I know. You don't have to say it." Bad news in Hollywood, like showing up unprepared for a major audition with a prominent director, traveled fast. If that happened, she could kiss her chances of ever being in a Holland Ainsley film, or Holland helping her with her future ambitions, goodbye.

Chapter Five

"Hold on, boy. We're almost done." Tristan patted the black gelding while the farrier, Wes, a thin older man with a smooth bald head who usually had a stoic expression on his deep brown face, secured the last of the four padded boots on the horse's right back hoof.

Jumping Jett started to fidget, and Tristan continued to soothe him. The gelding had come to Tillbridge yesterday from another boarding stable in Virginia. Someone there had cut his hooves too short. Not wanting to risk a crack or an infection, he'd called Wes and asked him to make a special Tuesday trip ahead of his usual Friday visit to check Jett out.

A few whinnies and soft snorts from the other horses echoed along with the hum of the ventilation system in the modern stable.

Grooms and helpers had mucked out the stalls early that morning and exercised their assigned horses. The horses boarding strictly in the surrounding pastures had been attended to, as well. Trainers had also finished working with their horses and conducting lessons with local clients. The busy morning had settled to a quiet afternoon. Temporarily. Basic lessons and trail rides for the guests would take up the rest of the day.

Once summer arrived in a couple of months, beating the heat would become a main priority. Trying to schedule stable activities before noon for the guests, when it was cooler, along with keeping up with the needs of their local clients and the horses, could potentially become a nightmare. That's why he and Zurie needed to seriously discuss the expansion.

Not only was a large indoor arena needed but also additional boarding stalls and new equipment for riders interested in learning how to ride English-style versus Western. As far as the cost, they could cover the expense by offering riding clinics in the indoor arena or offering it as a practice space for local competitors who participated in events like dressage and show jumping, or barrel racing and other rodeo events.

He knew exactly what needed to be done and how to do it. But just like yesterday morning before she'd left for the airport, Zurie kept setting aside their discussion about it.

Lately, she just seemed focused on the guesthouse and restaurant, which remained consistently booked with people who had an interest in horses and those who just wanted to experience a getaway from the city.

There were also more catered events happening on the property from kid's parties to wedding receptions to wine-tasting events.

He could see where amenity baskets, the catering menu and the thread count of the bedsheets could take up Zurie's time, but what about the rest of the operation? In his opinion, the comfort of the guests shouldn't override the needs of the horses. The prime reason owners in Maryland, Virginia and DC boarded their horses at Tillbridge Horse Stable, or more accurately the new name the operation had adopted six months ago, Tillbridge Horse Stable *and* Guesthouse, was for the expert care and training of their prized equines.

Wes closed the final strip of Velcro on the boot wrapped around Jett's hoof. "This will take the pressure off so it won't be painful for him to walk. No need to call the vet unless things get worse, but that shouldn't happen. Just use the specialized food and supplement protocol for him."

"Will do." Tristan glanced out the stall.

Pete, one of the helpers, was spraying down the wide rubber-floored aisle in between the stalls with a water hose. A few of the horses looking out the top part of the navy Dutch-style horizontally split doors watched him.

Tristan slipped his phone from his back jeans pocket and checked the time. Just after twelve. Most of the guests were having lunch at Pasture Lane. The rest of the grooms, helpers and trainers were probably taking advantage of the downtime grabbing food from the van, sent over by Philippa, parked near the outdoor seating area near the stable.

He motioned for Pete to come down to get Jett. The groom nodded a hello to Wes before leading the horse out the rear of the treatment area into the adjoining large fenced-in paddock. From there he'd walk Jett to the rear entrance of his stall.

Wes placed the hoof tester in his scuffed red tool-box. "I heard things are getting busier around here. I guess all the changes Zurie made are paying off."

"They are." But some days, it felt as if they were running a vacation resort or a theme park. Or maybe acting camp.

How could she think agreeing to have Chloe shadowing her—correction, shadowing him—was a good idea?

And as far as him being up to the task of running the stable and helping Chloe, she knew that had nothing to do with it, otherwise she wouldn't have made the decision to leave him in charge in the first place. His busy schedule was the issue and monitoring Chloe was adding to it. How could Chloe learn anything about the operation, anyway, if all she wanted to do was get away from the heart and soul of Tillbridge? The horses.

Wes's expression grew nostalgic as he continued to pack up his things. "You know, I remember when Mathew and your father partnered in opening this place. Years ago…"

Tristan knew Wes's often-told story well. Thirty years ago, the operation was just a few acres of land and three horses boarding in the pasture. His father, Jacob, and his uncle Mathew still had day jobs to pay the bills, and his aunt Cherie had taught riding lessons on weekends, even after Zurie and Rina were born.

Tristan nodded and smiled in all the right places as Wes went on. Sometimes he wondered if Wes had forgotten he was a Tillbridge and he was telling him the story about his family. Or at least part of the story. There was an extended, less tidy version that many people, including Wes, didn't know.

Jacob hadn't realized he was a father until Tristan's mother had shown up in Bolan with him when he was two years old. They'd married, and she'd stayed for a few months, but according to his father, she hadn't been able to take living in the "middle of nowhere" so she'd packed up a short time later, left Tristan behind, and hadn't come back. He didn't remember her.

Fatherhood had been a struggle for Jacob, and he'd stayed mainly on the periphery of Tristan's life. Mathew and Cherie had raised him like a son and Rina and Zurie were like his sisters. But Jacob had been the one to put him on a pony as soon as he'd been able to ride.

Images filtered through Tristan's mind of growing up in the large white clapboard home, where the guesthouse now stood, with his father, Uncle Mathew, Aunt Cherie, Rina and Zurie.

Following in Zurie's footsteps, he'd started competing in rodeos at the age of nine. That had prompted Jacob to take more of an interest in him. In his teens, when he'd started riding bulls, his father had even driven him to a few of his bigger competitions.

Wes chuckled, still wandering through the old days.

"I'm sure they never imagined the stable would grow into all of this."

Even at age thirty-two, the lesson Tristan had learned as a boy to respect his elders stuck with him. He tamped down the urge to interrupt and move Wes along. "Yes, we've definitely grown."

"You know, I'm not surprised about how successful Tillbridge has become. Zurie was always smart and she's just as strategy-minded as her father was. If Mathew and Cherie were still alive, I'm sure they would be proud of how hard she's worked to save this place from going under." He shot Tristan an apologetic look. "Not that you haven't had a hand in things."

Tristan could see hints of what the older man really believed about him in his eyes—that he'd had a hand in almost dismantling Tillbridge, not saving it. He'd been the one to abandon his family when they'd needed him most, trying to turn pro as a bull rider. And because he'd selfishly chased his dream, he'd gotten himself written out of his father's will, opening the door for Erica, his father's much younger second wife, to inherit ownership in Tillbridge.

When Jacob had died a little over two years ago, she hadn't given a damn about anything except getting the highest offer for her share of the stable. After several weeks of tense negotiations, Zurie had succeeded in buying back the shares from Erica before she'd sold them to someone else.

Wes picked up his toolbox. "While I'm here, I may as well check out the rest of the horses."

"I'd appreciate that. Let me know if you need anything."

As Tristan let Wes go ahead of him out the stall the truth screamed inside of him. He'd never abandoned his family or Tillbridge. He'd given up everything to protect them.

With Jumping Jett's checkup off his schedule, Tristan left Wes to check on the horses and went down the long hallway at the back of the stable. As he passed by a series of black and silver framed photos on the wall from the early days, mostly of his father and uncle competing in rodeos, Wes's bittersweet history lesson revived in his mind.

He paused in front of a photo of him at twenty years old with his father, arms wrapped around each other's shoulders and grinning as they held the large gold oval prize buckle for team calf roping. The event had always been his father's and Uncle Mathew's specialty, not his, but it had been Father's Day and a chance to share a special moment with his father before he'd left for army basic training. Winning had made that day even better.

How could they have known when that photo was taken that their family would experience more sadness than smiles over the next decade?

Like clockwork, heartache had shown up regularly on their doorstep. Aunt Cherie losing her life in a car accident. Rina almost dying in the same way. Mathew, who'd never gotten over losing the love of his life, inexplicably passing away in his sleep.

After her father died, Zurie had stepped up to take Mathew's place in actively running the stable with Jacob while Rina had chosen—and still did—to function as mainly a silent partner.

He'd promised Zurie he'd be there to help shoulder the responsibility of running the stable after his discharge from the military.

During those couple of years, he'd returned home on leave whenever possible, but there wasn't much he could do other than pitch in where needed, usually in the stable, for the few days he was around. Remembering those visits and knowing he had family and a place waiting for him had gotten him through some of his toughest tours in the Middle East. Months before he was supposed to come home for good, his father had married Erica.

I will not let you come between us...

That statement from his father during an argument had opened a wide rift between them. Meanwhile, Erica had stood by playing the victim, not caring that her actions had wrecked his and his father's relationship. He'd had to leave and break his promise to Zurie.

Tristan dropped his hand from the photo. A little over two years ago, he'd stood by his father's bedside in the hospital. He'd suffered a stroke. Erica had recently left him. His father had looked so fragile, as if he'd lost the will to fight, but they'd reconciled, privately in his hospital room, before he'd died. But not in time to change the will back for him to inherit ownership in Tillbridge or even his father's vintage collection of prize buckles. They also didn't get a chance to settle things as an entire family with Zurie and Rina there, too.

Turning from his memories, Tristan continued down the hall. By the time he'd reached the end of it, he'd packed away the grief in a box reserved for it in his mind and shut the lid tight.

In his shared office, smart windows along the wall on the left had darkened to a smoky-blue gray keeping the beige-tiled white-walled space cool. Outside, many of the staff were eating lunch along with a handful of guests and locals in a fenced-in eating area.

Gloria, the office administrator sat at her wood-topped metal desk along the opposite wall. Nothing was out of place on or around her, from her silver-streaked dark hair secured into a neat bun to her pressed Tillbridge shirt to the evenly stacked files and pens lined up on her desk. As a longtime employee at the stable who'd assisted his uncle, father and now him running the office, she had the ability to keep everyone in line with a single, direct look.

As she peered at him over her electric-blue–framed glasses, she removed a clip from a stack of papers and dropped it into a desk organizer. "How's Jett?"

"On the mend. We're using the specialized hoof care protocol for him. Can you put that in his file and add what we need for him to the supplement and feed orders?"

"Sure can, and I'll give his owner the update. Speaking of feeding—Philippa called about the Spring Fling cookout."

"Is there a problem?"

"Possibly. Zurie wanted Philippa to keep expenses in line with last year. She can keep the barbecued chicken on the menu, but she'll have to change the smoked prime rib that everyone loves to hamburgers. She also needs to know what the hours for Pasture Lane will be on that day. Is the restaurant closing at eleven right after breakfast or closing later after lunch?"

Last year, when they'd scheduled their annual Western-themed event for the staff, the guesthouse and the full-scale restaurant hadn't existed so they'd just closed the entire place that Wednesday to clients. There had also been fewer staff to feed.

"Ask her if she can maintain costs and keep the prime rib by cutting back on the appetizers or side dishes. The restaurant can close at eleven, but put it on our website and post a sign now so the regulars will know about the change. Also confirm if the last future occupancy report I saw the day of the Fling is still accurate. If it is, and we don't have anyone booked at the guesthouse that Wednesday, tell her to block it off from reservations. We'll resume regular business hours for the entire property on Thursday."

Gloria smiled her approval of his decisions as she handed him the feed report. "Will do."

Zurie might not be pleased about closing things down once she heard about it, but the Wednesday Spring Fling event had been a tradition for over two decades at Tillbridge for all staff members who'd wanted to attend. It provided a break as well as needed team-bonding time. Not giving everyone a chance to enjoy the entire afternoon, or Philippa's coveted prime rib, could dampen morale. As hard as everyone worked to make the operation a success, they deserved it.

Laughter drifting in from outside made him pause on the way to his desk at the back of the office. "When did lunch become so amusing?"

Gloria chuckled as she stacked papers on her desk. "My guess is it's not the food, but who's serving it."

"Who's out there?"

"I don't know, but I heard she's pretty."

He walked over and glanced out the window at the wood-corralled seating area a short walk from the stable.

The restaurant's lime green vehicle, taller and longer than the average van, sat parked under two large oak trees.

He couldn't see who was inside.

A few of the staff, mostly guys, lingered at the service window or sat at the picnic tables closer to it. Usually, they just grabbed their lunch and sat at the outer tables.

Curiosity and a bothersome suspicion drove him to lay the report on Gloria's desk, leave the office and walk out the side door.

He hadn't seen Chloe since she'd arrived yesterday, and Philippa hadn't called to complain about her so he'd assumed Chloe was into her research, and he didn't have to worry about her until next week or maybe not at all. She wouldn't risk sweating her makeup off working in a food van or messing up another pair of high heels. Would she?

As he got closer, the group hanging around the van scattered.

The lone woman framed by the side service window had her back to him. A green bandana held her dark curly ponytail in place.

That wasn't Chloe. Philippa must have forgotten to mention she'd hired someone new.

She faced him.

Chapter Six

Chloe suppressed a laugh in seeing the shock on Tristan's face. "Hi. What'll it be today? Turkey or ham?"

His surprise morphed to a suspicion-filled expression as his gaze narrowed on her.

"Not interested in sandwiches? Huh, let's see." She looked away from him a moment, feigning deep concern over his lack of enthusiasm for the lunch selections. "Maybe the beef stew, then? Blake and Adam said it was wonderful."

Upon hearing their names, at a nearby table, Blake, who she'd managed to coax a chuckle out of after telling the horse trainer he looked like Bradley Cooper, gave a semblance of a smile. Where he fell short, the ginger-haired, suntanned, just-a-minute-out-of-college

Adam, who worked as a groom at the stable, made up for it with a full-on grin.

"We need to talk. Open the door." Tristan stalked to the other side of the van.

What was he so irritated about? Probably the fact that they were simply breathing air in the same space.

A mischievous glee sparked in Chloe that just her presence needled him. Between growing up verbally sparring with an older brother, who she now loved, but who had been a terrorizing brat when they were younger, and having endured everything from pain-in-the-ass actors high on fame to directors losing it because Mother Nature had the nerve to rain down on their perfect scene, she was more than prepared for him. And Tristan deserved some pushback for ignoring her and being a pain in the butt about helping her out.

She wiped away her pleased smile, took a cleansing breath and slid open the door. Before she'd had a chance to say "Come on in," he'd stepped inside, and the van that had once been stable slightly rocked under her feet.

Partway down the narrow aisle separating the freezer/fridge combo from the food table warming the beef stew, he stopped and faced her. "What do you think you're doing?"

"Last time I checked, it was called working."

"If your idea of research is practicing your acting skills on my staff while pretending to work, you can stop now."

Pretending? Was she pretending when she'd burned her fingers putting food into the heating table? Or what about the stains that were never coming out of her favorite white Misha Nonoo tee she'd put on that morning for a lack of anything else to wear?

Calm gave way to irritation. "Last time I checked, the food I helped prepare and stock in this van was real, and the only skill I've practiced for the past half hour is making sure everyone is happy with lunch. In fact, we were all extremely happy until you showed up with your problem, whatever that may be."

"Damn right I have a problem."

"Oh, really? I can't wait to hear it."

He advanced. "Let's start with you being impatient and not waiting until I got back to you with a plan about where you should be while you're here."

"You mean me being proactive."

She took a step, putting mere inches between them, but something curiously appealing about the scowl on his face short-circuited the rest of her response.

He had the best brooding man pout ever. She'd worked with an actor who'd taken endless selfies trying to pull that look off, but he'd reached only the 101 level in that department. Tristan had it mastered naturally to the level of flat-out sexy. What would he do if she reenacted that scene from her television past and kissed his pout away?

As if he'd read her mind, Tristan's gaze momentarily dropped to her mouth. When his eyes met hers, the challenge in his wasn't scripted. It was real, filled with pure confidence, and devoid of arrogance.

Did he honestly think she wouldn't do it? The prospect of answering his silent dare sparked excitement.

A knock echoed in the van.

Chloe and Tristan both stepped back.

Needing to focus on something other than Tristan, she looked over her shoulder.

A woman in a lavender T-shirt who resembled Zurie, except that she was taller and had thin braids gathered in a yellow hair band, stood at the door holding a metal tray of pies. She glanced down at the load in her hands, "A little help here, please."

"Of course." Chloe hurried over to her and took the rack. Philippa had mentioned someone from Brewed Haven, the café Zurie's sister owned, was dropping off desserts.

Limited space required her to pass the tray to Tristan who slid it into a rack built into the back of the van.

"It's time for the amateur to leave and make room for the professionals." The Zurie look-alike who she assumed was Rina gestured for someone to get out.

Tristan looked to Chloe.

"Not her, you." The woman pointed to him. "But before you go to your office, make yourself useful. I have two more trays in my car."

Tristan shot her a look, but Zurie's sister stared him down. Resignation replaced his annoyed expression. "Give me the keys."

Chloe maneuvered partially between the driver and passenger seats to make room for him to get out. Tristan taking orders. Oh, she liked this woman a lot.

He took the keys and clomped away from the van.

The woman got in. "Men." She exaggerated exasperation. "Hi, I'm Zurie's sister, Rina. You must be Chloe."

"Yes, I am. You really need to teach me how to do that thing you just did with Tristan."

Rina laughed. "He knows better than to argue with me. I keep him supplied with his favorite dessert."

Before Chloe could ask what that was, a woman and her young child came to the window. In the midst of serving the canned sodas and pretzel the woman ordered, a long line started to form.

It was the lunch rush Philippa had mentioned—guests and locals who wanted snacks and grab-and-go meals.

Chloe rubbed her damp palms down her apron. She'd been planning to go over the van checklist a few more times, but she'd been too busy arguing with Tristan.

Rina nudged her. "I'm sticking around. Philippa asked me to give you a hand."

A breath of relief surged out of Chloe. "Thanks." She might survive, after all, even if she hadn't gotten a chance to memorize every step.

She and Rina worked in tandem, serving and ringing up orders. At some point, Tristan brought the other trays of desserts but she didn't see him. Rina opening and slamming the door shut marked his arrival and departure.

A little over an hour later, the line diminished to a few intermittent stragglers.

"Whew!" Chloe stepped away from the window and fanned her face, trying to create a breeze. "That was intense. I'm so glad you were here."

"You did well for your first time in the van." Rina

grabbed two bottles of water from the fridge and handed one to her. "A lot of people wimp out under the pressure."

"Thanks." Pride in accomplishing another major task on only her second day at Tillbridge welled inside of her. Chloe opened the bottle and took a long sip. Her throat was dry from talking to customers and communicating their orders to Rina. "I'm sure Tristan will be shocked to hear I could handle it."

"What's going on with you and him anyway? It looked like the two of you were in the midst of a face-off when I walked up."

"Wish I knew." Whatever had happened between her and Tristan earlier before Rina arrived, Chloe honestly couldn't explain it. One minute, they were arguing and then… "Maybe it's because Zurie told him he has to show me around while she's gone. I'm an actress, and I'm here researching for an audition. I was supposed to shadow her."

"I heard about that. She left, he got stuck with you and then he dropped you in Philippa's lap." Rina's expression turned slightly sheepish. "Sorry, I didn't mean to sound harsh."

"But it's the truth, and there's nothing I can do to change it. He's against me in every way."

"Against you. Seriously?" Rina tilted her head to the side and studied her. "Maybe it's not you but someone else."

"No. I'm sure it's me. He's made it perfectly clear he thinks I shouldn't be here, but that's okay. I've handled worse, and I'm only here for a few weeks. After that, neither one of us will have to see each other again."

Rina's cell chimed and she took it from her back jeans pocket and checked the screen. "I've got to head back to the café soon. Did Tristan eat?"

"Not anything from here."

"He never misses lunch, especially when there's lemon meringue pie. I'll take him something." Rina grabbed the last wrapped ham sandwich from the fridge and a slice of apple pie on a small paper plate wrapped in plastic.

"Wait." Chloe pointed. "There's one more slice of lemon in the back."

"I know, and I think you deserve it for working so hard." Rina handed her the slice of lemon pie.

Laughing, Chloe accepted the plate of dessert. "If I must."

"Yes, you must. Lunch is over. Take a break and eat it before you head back to the restaurant."

While Rina delivered the food, Chloe stowed and secured a few remaining items in the van.

The pie beckoned.

She really should have something more than just pie, but Rina was right. She did deserve a treat.

Chloe stripped off her apron, grabbed a plastic fork and went outside.

In the vacant seating area, a few napkins, cans and bottles hadn't found their way into the portable trash bins.

She'd get to them in a minute. Weariness and a lingering sense of achievement dropped down with Chloe on the bench at the table. She'd experienced a feeling of achievement after acing a scene in a show or movie, but this felt different. Probably because she'd faced down Tristan.

The remembered image of him, staring down at her just as she'd thought about lifting on her toes and pressing her lips to his, bloomed in her mind. What would have happened if she'd boldly taken possession of his mouth or would he have won the sensual duel and taken ownership of hers instead?

Chloe took a bite of delicious pie and mulled over the question. She didn't know the answer, but she wished she would have found out.

Chapter Seven

Tristan pecked and stabbed the computer keyboard, trying to stay focused on the expense report, but his internal clock kept counting down the minutes, reminding him that the food van was leaving soon. And then there was the issue of his growling stomach. Normally, there were snacks in the corner minifridge, but today there was only water. No food. He was surviving on just coffee.

He'd contemplated asking Gloria to grab him something before she left to run errands, but she would have looked at him as if he'd suddenly sprouted two heads. Getting lunch for him wasn't in her job description. He could go to Pasture Lane or Brewed Haven Café. But then that would raise questions from Philippa or

Rina about why he'd changed his usual pattern and not grabbed food from the van.

He'd made it through firefights in the army and taken on tough bulls in bull-riding competitions. He should have been able to walk outside and get a sandwich, but Chloe smiling at him as if she'd won the battle about being there would have gotten under his skin. She hadn't. He just should have been more specific with Philippa about how to keep Chloe preoccupied until his schedule freed up. Having her in the vicinity of the stable, right now, with her discomfort around horses, and stirring up memories of Zurie's ultimatum that he had to look after her, was a distraction he didn't need…along with the problem of almost kissing her.

It didn't make sense. Actually, it did. She had a mouth perfect for instigating an argument and even more perfect for kissing. At least that's what his mind kept telling him along with prompting him to test that theory out.

His cell buzzed on his desk with an incoming text message. It was from Zurie.

Everything okay there?

This was the fourth time she'd checked in since yesterday. Lately, she was doing that more and more. What was up with her? Maybe she didn't think he could handle things. It was the first time she'd left him in charge since the guesthouse opened. Did she really believe that after almost two years of proving himself, he'd just slack off?

How are things with Chloe?

Aside from her distracting him from work and keeping him from a good meal. Nothing at all. Thanks for asking. He responded.

All good. Busy. Talk later.

He dropped the phone on his desk and went back to typing.

"Tapping the keys works just as well as stabbing at them." Rina walked into his office carrying a wrapped sandwich and pie.

His mouth watering drowned his retort.

She set the food in front of him.

He tore open the sandwich and took a bite. Smoky ham combined with the nutty flavor of homemade whole grain bread danced over his taste buds.

Rina dropped into the black-padded chair in front of his desk. "You're welcome."

"I was about to say thank you. Did you run out of lemon meringue pie?"

"Almost. I gave the last piece to Chloe." She pointed at him and circled her finger in the air. "And that ugly look that just took over your face, along with your attitude, is why she deserved it more than you did."

"The only reason I have this look on my face is because you just told me you gave away my slice of pie."

"Deny it all you want, but it doesn't seem that way to me. When I walked up to the van, it sounded like you were arguing with her, and when Gloria stopped by to grab lunch, she told me that you were in a bad mood, *and* she seemed to think Chloe had something to do with it. What's up with you?"

He answered between bites. "It's hectic. I've got horses transferring in from other stables that need special care, supplies being delivered later than expected, the south pasture gate needs a full replacement instead of just a new lock, and because of that pasture management is now delayed. Then the guesthouse has its own set of issues, something about not enough bath bombs for the VIP amenity baskets. Oh, and a tight budget. We may not have prime rib for Spring Fling if Philippa can't shave a few dollars elsewhere from the menu."

"And I'm guessing Zurie's unexpected departure is adding to your frustration?" Rina's faint smile meant she already knew the answer to that question.

Tristan set the sandwich on his desk. "It's not so much about her deciding not to be here for a month. Don't get me wrong, a heads-up of more than a half hour before she left for the airport would have been nice, but it's all of the changes to the operation that's bothering me. We're barely keeping up with them. And she still won't talk about the expansion plan, and in the midst of all of this, she not only leaves but hands me the bigger problem of babysitting an actress?"

Rina huffed a chuckle. "Well, if Chloe's your biggest problem, you need more like her. After the way she handled the van during lunch, she deserves a standing ovation."

"I'm sure she'd love the attention." He took another bite of his sandwich.

"Why do you say that?"

"Aren't actresses naturally the attention-seeking type?"

"I don't know about other actresses, but that's not how she came across to me. Are you really seeing her or is she reminding you of someone else?"

"Who?"

"Erica."

The mention of his father's widow stole the pleasing taste from the food in his mouth. He swallowed. "Why bring her into this?"

"Because when I first walked up to the van and saw Chloe, for a second, she reminded me of her, and Erica did take acting lessons."

He'd forgotten about Erica's dream of taking over Hollywood.

His father had indulged her, paying for acting lessons that had required her to fly back and forth from Maryland to New York every week. But when Erica's feelings had gotten hurt by criticism, she'd quit, and his father had cheered her up with a shopping spree. Clothes, jewelry, a fully loaded red sports convertible—what Erica wanted, Erica got...except for one thing. And that refusal had almost completely destroyed his relationship with his father.

Tristan pushed the half-eaten sandwich away. "I still don't see your point in bringing her into this."

"Maybe you're making some subliminal connection between the two of them."

No way. He was trying to sever any connections with Erica influencing his life, not make new ones. As he drank the last of the coffee in his mug, the tepid temperature along with the bitter dregs made him grimace. "No, it's just that Chloe's arrival is really bad timing."

"And that's not her fault."

"Which brings me back to *my* original point. Zurie is the cause, and part of me wonders if she's purposely pushing my buttons."

"Oh, please, you know Zurie isn't into wasting time cooking up petty bull crap. She's just really adamant about doing things her way, but deep down, she means well. Most of all, she wants the best for Tillbridge."

"The best thing for Tillbridge is for her to be more open to suggestions about running it."

"I know, but..." Rina shrugged. "All I can say is give her time." She stood and picked up his empty mug.

Her walking with a barely perceptible limp to the coffee maker stalled his response. Undoubtedly, she'd been up before dawn overseeing breakfast prep at her café. She needed to rest her knee, but if he said that, Rina would only remind him of how he'd kept riding bulls through his own sometimes agonizing injuries.

For him there was no shame in popping a couple of pain relievers and taking a pause, even now when old aches revisited him on chilly days. But Rina never admitted when she was hurting, and having someone else notice seemed to make her think people saw her as helpless or weak.

Unable to accept her waiting on him, he got up and went to her.

Despite the discomfort she was feeling, as she handed him the mug, she gave him an empathetic smile. "I know you're frustrated with Zurie right now, but why torture yourself? In less than a couple of months, you'll have what you wanted."

What he'd worked two years to get from Zurie— ownership in Tillbridge.

After Zurie had succeeded in getting his father's share of the stable from Erica, he'd offered to buy it from Zurie. She could have sold it directly to him, but she'd chosen to follow the bylaw she'd instituted, right after the Erica inheritance incident, making two successive years of management experience as a requirement before being eligible for ownership in Tillbridge. Two years. The amount of time wasn't lost on him. She was upset at him and it was clearly a loyalty test. But to get what he wanted, he'd had no choice but to set aside his disappointment, take the stable manager position she'd offered him and prove his worthiness, as an employee.

Honestly, if the situation had been turned around, and he'd been in her shoes, believing what she thought about him, he might have done the same.

Tristan looked to Rina and the hopefulness for the future that he saw in her eyes unearthed a bit of sadness inside of him. "Sure, soon I'll have part ownership in Tillbridge, but signatures on a legal document won't magically transform my relationship with Zurie. As long as she thinks I don't love this place as much as the two of you do, she'll doubt my every move."

Rina laid her hand on his. "Someday, she'll see it, but that definitely won't happen if you give her a reason to think that way. In the past two years, you've never failed to complete a task she's given you. Don't start now."

He followed Rina's gaze to the window where she glanced at Chloe sitting at one of the picnic tables probably enjoying his dessert. Ownership in Tillbridge was the priority, and right now, that included keeping her out of trouble. But mentally, he was too damn tired to sort out what to do with Chloe now. If she liked working in the food van, she could stay there until he got back to her next week, like he'd planned.

Tristan wrapped an arm around Rina's shoulders prompting her to lean against him as he gave her a squeeze. "You're right. Now isn't the time to give Zurie a reason to kick me out."

"Kick you out?" Rina swatted his chest. "Yeah, right. You're here forever with the rest of us and you know it. Team Tillbridge, forever."

Team Tillbridge. That's what Uncle Mathew used to say to them when they were kids right before they were about to dig in together to do things like shovel snow on the property, clean the stable from top to bottom or compete in a rodeo event. He'd never lost sight of what was important—family and Tillbridge Stable. Unfortunately, his father had.

Out of everyone, Rina was the only one who didn't seem to blame him for the mess his father's decision had caused. He did.

His rift with Jacob, getting written out of his will, breaking his promise to Zurie, possibly even his father's death might not have happened so soon if he hadn't made the one mistake that had put the wheels in motion.

He'd brought Erica home with him to Tillbridge.

Chapter Eight

Chloe adjusted the towels she'd folded into the shape of a horse and set it next to the VIP basket in the middle of the bed. After multiple attempts, she'd finally gotten the hang of it. Sort of. At least now the folded towel resembled a cute creature instead of a sad-looking blob. "How's that?"

"Great." Deanna, the housekeeping supervisor, smiled at her from the other side of the bed. "All that's left now is dusting and vacuuming." The middle-aged redhead plumped the white pillows against the padded beige headboard for the third time, straightened the basket, then adjusted the white pleated lamp shade on the wall lamp above the right-hand bedside table. She reminded Chloe of a constantly moving hummingbird.

"I'm going to walk through the rest of the cottage to see what needs to be done."

"I'll keep going in here." Chloe ran a duster over the bedside table and the dresser across from the bed that was underneath a flat screen television.

Lena would have a fit if she found out that after their talk three days ago, she still wasn't hanging out in the stable with the horses. But like she'd told Lena, pitching in at the restaurant, and now with housekeeping in the cleaning of the guesthouse and cottages, was actually helping her cause.

Chloe finished dusting and moved on to the one housekeeping task she hated—vacuuming. And just like at her apartment, somehow, she managed to get the cord tangled and stuck under the legs of the furniture.

She definitely wouldn't be doing the most boring housekeeping chore on earth if she didn't owe Deanna. When Philippa had mentioned to Deanna that Chloe needed to learn about horses, Deanna had contacted Adam. Like more than a few of the staff at the stable, they were related. He was her nephew. Now Chloe was all set up to spend time with Adam on his days off and after his shifts to learn more about horses. Once that arrangement had been made, how could she not volunteer that morning when Deanna asked for help?

But, honestly, it wasn't just about returning Deanna's favor. The staff had started to treat her like one of the group and it felt nice. A few of them had even invited her to happy hour that night to celebrate the end of the workweek. No, going out with them for drinks wasn't providing specific information about the Tillbridge operation, but she appreciated them including her. She was starting to gain their respect. And she'd done it without Tristan.

Chloe turned off the vacuum as Deanna came back into the bedroom. "What's next?"

"You just need to tidy up the kitchen and the living room. After that, you can move on to the other five cottages. I'm going back to the guesthouse."

"Wait. You want me to finish five more cottages on my own—but I'm still getting the hang of things."

"Don't panic." Deanna laughed. "You've done great so far, and you have plenty of time to get it done. Check-in for the cottages isn't until two, and that's in six hours. And you don't have to clean the last cottage, just stock the master bath with a week's worth of fresh towels." She handed Chloe a folded map. "I marked it so you'll know which one it is." Deanna gave her a reassuring smile before she walked out. "Call or give a shout on the radio if something comes up."

"Okay." Chloe spoke to the empty room as she tucked the map in the back pocket of her jeans.

Following the instructions Deanna had given her, as well as double-checking the housekeeping checklist, she continued cleaning her way forward up the hall to the guest bedroom and bath. Then she tackled the small kitchen and dining room, along with the living room before vacuuming her way out the door.

Close to one in the afternoon, she finished the fourth cottage. For an amateur, with only a few hours of experience, she'd done okay, and with more practice, she'd be able to do it perfectly. But she wouldn't trade working in the van for housekeeping. She'd missed talking to everyone, especially Adam, Blake and Gloria…and annoying Tristan.

He'd been out of the office the second day she'd worked in the food van. Yesterday, he'd walked to the van as if expecting, no hoping, not to see her there, then he'd ordered lunch with as few words as possible. She'd handed him his food, including a slice of lemon pie before he'd asked for it, and he'd gone back to his office. She could only imagine his reaction once he found out about her arrangement with Adam. But like Lena had reminded her, she had a larger objective that didn't include what Tristan thought about her. She couldn't allow him or his unwillingness to help to become a distraction.

Wanting to stretch her legs without lugging around the large wheeled cleaning cart filled with supplies, Chloe grabbed four sets of beige towels and walked down the main path. The last cottage was at the end of an offshoot to the left.

Using a master key card, she opened the door to a different setup than the other cottages. In place of carpeting, polished wood floors expanded throughout the space and cream window shades versus curtains hung partially down over the three front windows. The standard decor of beige living room furniture had been replaced with a buttery soft-looking brown leather couch and fabric-upholstered side chairs that formed a seating area around a glass-topped wood coffee table.

Ahead of her, in the one-wall kitchen, a pottery vase filled with kitchen utensils sat on the counter next to the stove where an emerald dish towel hung from the handle of the oven. Notes hung on the refrigerator door. All homey touches. The desk with a laptop and papers on top, pushed against the wall in the space normally designated as the dining area, confirmed someone lived there on a more permanent basis.

She went down a short beige carpeted hallway to the left between the living room and the kitchen. Walking past a closed door on the left, and a small bathroom on the right, she headed straight into the master bedroom. A king-size bed covered by a dove-gray comforter and slate-colored pillows dominated the space, and a faint woodsy scent hung in the air.

She'd encountered it before but where?

A black cowboy hat and silver-framed photos sat on a wood dresser on the wall near the footboard of the bed. All she had to do was walk over, take a peek, and find out the answer. No. That was snooping. She was just supposed to drop off fresh towels, pick up the used ones and leave.

Chloe marched straight into the connecting bathroom. She set the towels on the white marble counter next to a small round tin of shaving soap and a shaving brush, intending to pick up the plastic bag of laundry on the floor near the corner shower and leave. But as if something had given them an invisible nudge, the towels toppled, knocking the tin into the sink.

After righting the stack, she picked up the small round container that had popped open. Most guys just used shaving cream in a can. Unable to resist, she lifted it to her nose and breathed in the clean wonderful smell reminiscent of rich earth, fresh pine...*and cooling summer rain*. It was definitely Tristan's scent.

The sound of a door opening and closing at the rear of the cottage echoed.

Was that Deanna coming to check on her?

She put the closed tin next to the shaving brush. Noticing several slivers of soap dotting the sink, she turned on the water. Using her hand to push them toward the drain, she rinsed them away.

Tristan's voice drifted down the hall. "I didn't forget about the meeting. I just got back from the new gate install in the south pasture. I need to clean up and change."

Shit! After double-checking that everything was in its place, Chloe hurriedly picked up the bag of dirty towels. She walked out the bedroom...just in time to witness him unbuttoning his navy shirt as he came out of the kitchen. The gradual reveal of his defined chest took precedence over moving her feet. *Wow.* He was all kinds of droolworthy, and she was ogling him... making that all kinds of wrong.

Giving herself a mental shake, she avoided looking at him and hurried toward the front door. "Towels." His one-word way of communicating had definitely rubbed off on her.

Just as she reached for the knob, he called out. "You dropped something."

She faced him. He was close. Close enough for her to breathe in the faint smell of the woodsy soap now pleasingly mixed with a hint of hardworking man. Near enough to cause her heart to race a thousand and one beats per minute as she got a good look at his defined chest. His partially unbuttoned shirt revealed a tempting peek at the first row of what promised to be endless chiseled abs.

It took effort to force her attention on the property map in his hand. "Oh. It slipped out of my pocket." She took hold of it.

But Tristan wouldn't let go. A questioning expression came over his face as he sniffed the air.

Moments passed before she caught a whiff of the problem. The scent of his shaving soap lingered on her hand. She hadn't been nosing around his things, the tin just fell into the sink. "The towels knocked it over."

His brows came together as he looked at her.

"Your shaving soap. It fell into the sink and I had to wash it down the drain… I mean pieces of it." Her inability to form coherent sentences tipped her even higher on the embarrassment meter with Tristan's puzzled expression and her inability to keep her eyes off his hard chest. If only she could have swum down the drain along with his soap.

"Going." Chloe turned away from him. She was really starting to appreciate caveman-speak. She couldn't mess it up.

"Don't you still want this?"

An image of Tristan and his promised abs sprang up. Darn right she did, but that wasn't what he was talking about. *The map*… He still had it.

Just grab the thing and don't stare. Chloe whirled around. She avoided looking into his eyes, but the rest of him… A sigh of appreciation slipped out.

"No." Chloe snatched the paper from him and shook her head, emphasizing the point more for herself than him. "Distraction. Bad. Very bad."

Chapter Nine

Tristan sat at the bar counter in the semicrowded space attached to the Montecito Steakhouse just outside of town. He half watched the recap of last night's basketball game on one of the huge flat screens above the bar in front of him.

As he took a pull from his bottle of beer, the remembered image of Chloe snatching the paper from his hand at the cottage that afternoon, then shutting the door in his face, wove into his thoughts. Distraction—bad? Had she been referring to him? She was the one who'd invaded his space.

Raucous conversation grew louder at the table where Chloe sat sharing last call happy hour drinks with a group of staff from Tillbridge.

And she was still doing it. After she'd left, all he'd

kept thinking about was how much he'd liked smelling the scent of his shaving soap on Chloe. Tristan ran his hand over the shadow of hair on his jawline. Staying away from his razor for the next few days would probably be a good idea. He didn't trust his concentration.

Rina had claimed his problem was that Chloe reminded him of Erica. He could honestly say that wasn't true. He'd definitely never wanted to kiss Erica, and Chloe wasn't a spoiled pain. She was just damn persistent about getting what she wanted, and actually, he could respect that. He was just as determined when it came to working toward what mattered to him. But Erica didn't share that quality. She just expected people to give her what she wanted. Too bad he hadn't picked up on that when he'd met her.

He and Erica had been seated next to each other in the same row on a flight from Atlanta to Baltimore. At the time he'd been six months away from the end of his enlistment. Flying to Maryland from where he'd been stationed in Georgia had served a dual purpose—spend Memorial Day weekend with his family and speak with his father to establish where he might fit in at the stable once he'd been discharged and came home for good.

The casual conversation he'd struck up with Erica had started when he'd asked if she had enough room in the center seat, an attempt to give a hint to the guy sitting near the window that he was manspreading all over her. As they'd kept talking, she'd mentioned moving to DC because she'd wanted a change of pace from where she lived in Augusta.

After they'd landed, she'd gotten a message from

the friend who was supposed to pick her up. They'd decided to leave town for the weekend and had forgotten to leave her a key to the apartment she was sharing with them.

As she'd stood in the baggage claim area waiting for her luggage, she'd reminded him of an abandoned foal, cute but lost and looking for someplace to go. Feeling sorry for her, he'd given her a ride to a hotel and then invited her to spend the holiday with him and his family.

Chloe's carefree laugh teased him from the past. No. She was nothing like Erica. She was capable of finding her own way, and especially now, she looked good doing it. The white fitted tee and pink jeans she had on clung to her in all the right places. She just needed his Stetson to go with those cowboy boots she was wearing. His Stetson? Wait. Where had that come from?

Something was said at her table causing everyone to snicker and hoot in response.

Adam, who sat beside Chloe, pushed up the sleeves of his gray shirt, then casually laid his arm on the back of her chair.

An hour ago, when he was leaving the office for the day, Gloria had informed him that Deanna had told her Adam was going to teach Chloe about horses. She'd said it while peering at him over her glasses, with an expression that had made him feel like he was ten years old and had disappointed her by not completing some expected task.

He'd meant to tell Chloe his plan about catching up with her next week. But with attending business commerce association meetings in Bolan and Baltimore in Zurie's place, and handling the arrival of new horses along with everything else, it honestly skipped his mind. But once again she'd found her own way, eliminating his problem. So why wasn't he thrilled about it?

"Hey." Mace settled into the stool beside him, off duty and casual in a tan long-sleeved pullover and jeans. He signaled to the bartender to bring two of the beers Tristan was drinking. "Are you just going to stare at her or buy her a drink?"

Was he that obvious? Damn. Tristan put his attention back on the flat screen. "Plenty of people are buying her drinks. She doesn't need one from me."

At least three different guys had sent cocktails her way during happy hour, but after accepting the drinks, she hadn't opened the door to introductions. She'd just politely acknowledged the senders, then surreptitiously passed the cocktails to her tablemates.

Mace chuckled. "Looks like the former high school quarterback is calling his play. I give Adam credit for trying, but he's way out of his league with her. By the way, what's her name?"

"Chloe Daniels."

"So she's staying at the guesthouse?"

"Yeah."

"And?"

"And what?"

"Why is she here?" Mace took one of the beers the bartender dropped off and slid the other one to Tristan.

"She's an actress researching a part for some movie.

Zurie was supposed to help her out, but she left town, and now I'm stuck with her."

"An actress, huh?" Mace's brow raised with interest. "You know, I think I recognize her. I'll have to look her up. Have you seen any of her shows or movies?"

"No."

"What's the name of the movie she's auditioning for?"

"I don't know. Does it matter?"

"It might. Why are you looking at me like it's a dumb question?" Mace shrugged. "Maybe I'll want to see it."

Tristan tamped down annoyance and turned his attention to his beer. He'd thought at least Mace would see things from his point of view when it came to the Chloe situation. Zurie hadn't given him a choice, just dictated terms.

Mace pointed to the far wall. "Dartboard's free. You up for a game?"

He was up for anything that changed the subject and got Chloe off his mind. "I'm always up for beating you."

"Whatever lies get you through the night."

They both took their beers and ambled to the far side of the room, but just before they got to the board, Adam stepped up. "There's a waiting list. Blake and I are next."

Had Chloe finally gotten tired of Adam and kicked him to the curb? From the self-assured look on his face, probably not. Maybe it was time to take him down a notch in a dart game.

"Why don't we team up?" Tristan gestured between himself and Mace. "Us against you and Blake."

"Sounds good to me." Adam pulled the darts from the board.

"Let's do this." Mace set his beer on a nearby tall table. "You owe us a basket of hot wings when you lose."

"Don't get too confident." Adam glanced behind Mace and Tristan. "Looks like there's been a change-up. Maybe Blake isn't playing."

Tristan looked back and spotted Chloe walking toward them. "Oh, hell no." The murmured words slipped past his lips, but Mace and Adam were too caught up in staring at her to notice.

She sauntered over to Adam's side carrying what looked to be a mojito. "Blake's busy so I'm taking his place. The server who brought our drinks is taking a dinner break, and he's going with her." Chloe exchanged a laugh and a knowing look with Adam. "I guess the pep talk I gave him about smiling at her worked."

Tristan took a swig of beer. She'd convinced Blake, who barely spoke to anyone, to take relationship advice? Charming Adam was one thing but Blake, too?

Mace thumped Tristan's arm. "You good?"

"Perfect."

"So which style are we playing?" Chloe didn't spare Tristan a glance as she set her glass next to Mace's on the tall table, then slipped a dart from Adam's hand. She walked up to the toe line and threw it at the board.

Chapter Ten

The dart hit the bull's-eye.

Chloe couldn't hold back a smile as she took in the mix of appreciative to slightly shocked expressions from Tristan, Adam and the guy Adam had told her earlier was named Mace.

Adam looked to her and said, "I say we play a standard 701 game since we're teaming up."

"I agree." She'd played that way before. Each team would start with 701 points, and each player would take turns throwing three darts. Their scores would be deducted from the totals. The first team to reduce the score to zero would win.

"Will that work for you?" Adam asked Mace and Tristan. "Unless you've changed your minds about playing against us."

"We're ready." Mace snagged a dart from the table. "We'll even let her throw count in determining which team goes first." He went to the toe line. His throw hit outside the bull's-eye.

Adam smirked. "In case you're wondering, I prefer Cajun over hot wings."

"Good to know." Tristan's bring-it-on look came with a dismissive snort. "Be sure to tell that to the server when you're using your own money to buy them." At the toe line, Tristan loosened up by rotating his wide shoulders.

As he took a throwing stance, Chloe's attention riveted on his tight-looking butt. A rush of warmth made her fan her face. Why was she flushed after just one mojito? She dragged her gaze from Tristan and ran into Mace's direct stare across the table. From his amused expression, he'd caught her staring at Tristan. More heat gathered in her cheeks.

Mace's amber gaze continued studying her as he drank from his beer. "We haven't formally met. I'm Mace." He moved over and stood beside her.

"Hi, I'm Chloe."

"You threw that bull's-eye without breaking a sweat. Who taught you to play? Your dad, a sister or brother, your boyfriend?"

Typical smooth move if the dark-haired deputy was fishing to see if she was single. She recognized him from when she'd stumbled that first morning at the stable. But it didn't feel like he was flirting with her, more like playing wingman. For who? Tristan? If he was, he must have missed the unhappy look on Tristan's face when she'd walked up and told them she was playing instead of Blake.

As a server slipped up beside her and dropped off a full platter of loaded fries, Chloe answered him. "I learned while filming a pilot episode for a series."

"So did they hire someone to teach you?"

Tristan came to the table and stood on the other side of Chloe. He nodded at Mace. "We're starting first. You're up."

"In a sec. Chloe was about to tell me who taught her how to play darts."

Both men zeroed their attention on her just as she ate a fry.

A bit self-conscious, sandwiched between them, under their direct stares, she took a much-needed sip from her glass to wash it down. "We were filming a scene in a bar, like this one, a few of the extras and I were supposed to play darts in the background. Technical issues delayed the scene, and while we waited, the extras taught me how to play."

"Oh?" Tristan grabbed some fries. "Who knew pretending for a living had a useful payoff."

"Pretending?"

Just before she was about to deliver a snappy comeback, she saw his faint smile. Tristan may have had opinions about her career, but he didn't come across as the type who was mean enough to embarrass her in front of people. No, this was about him wanting to win. He thought he could actually get into her head? Game on.

Chloe smiled sweetly. "You're right. Some of us do

have to pretend, at times." She slid a couple of napkins in front of him. "You should take these."

Tristan frowned. "Why? Do I have food on my mouth?"

"No, but you'll need them when you pretend not to cry after Adam and I kick your butts."

"Daaamn!" Mace playfully cringed as he backed his way to the toe line for his turn. "She burned you so bad that hurt me."

"I guess." Tristan's tone held amusement and grudging respect as he looked to Chloe. "Hope you can back your play, Ace."

"I can." She plucked a fry from the platter. "Can you?"

"Definitely. I don't run away from heated situations even when things get bad or distracting."

Throwing her words in her face from when she'd left his cottage. Oh, now he was playing dirty. She didn't run…exactly, but she'd had her reasons. They began and ended with her wanting to finish unbuttoning his shirt, and Chloe swallowed those reasons covered in cheese, bacon and sour cream. She could never tell him that.

But Tristan's knowing smile practically accused her of being a coward, and she couldn't resist wiping it from his face. "Distractions are just a minor detail." She feigned indifference. "As far as heated situations, I haven't encountered anything or anyone hot enough to make me run."

Tristan said something to her, but cheers for a soccer game playing on one of the flat screens drowned out his words. "What did you say?"

As he leaned closer, the woodsy scent she'd come to really like surrounded her. His hair-shadowed cheek rasped lightly over hers. "I said, are you sure about that?"

Obstinacy made her turn her head to look at him. Meeting him eye to eye with his mouth inches from hers, jumbled certainty. All that remained was curiosity. If Tristan kissed her would he boldly take possession of her mouth or use the slow sweeps of his lips to coax her into kissing him back? Not that she'd need a whole lot of persuading. A vision bloomed in her mind of them indulging in that latter kiss, and of it deepening and becoming more intense as desire took hold.

As if he'd read her mind, he leaned in and she did, too. Her heart echoed in her ears with the closing of inches to millimeters filled with anticipation and heat.

"Uh… Chloe." Adam standing across the table yanked her and Tristan back. "It's your turn, but if you're not playing anymore because…" The tips of his ears reddened as he looked from her to Tristan as if he was unsure of what to say.

Mace joined them. "Who's not doing what anymore?"

"Nothing." Chloe and Tristan interjected at the same time.

"Okay." Mace regarded all three of them with a level stare. "What did I miss?"

Adam's mouth opened then shut.

Tristan remained silent and turned his attention to the flat screens at the bar as he drank his beer.

The way Mace looked at her, as if he was conducting official business, made Chloe feel like she needed to confess, but to what? Nothing had happened.

"I'm up." Chloe snagged three darts from the table. Despite her sweat-slicked hands, she'd still managed to hit the board…barely.

When she returned, she braced to see triumph in Tristan's eyes for succeeding in throwing her off her game, but his focus stayed on the flat screens while Mace harassed Adam about needing to buy more bar food.

On the way to take his turn, Tristan's face revealed nothing about his strategy or what had happened between them a minute ago, but her traitorous heart kicked in a few extra beats. And why should she expect to see some sort of a reaction. Like they'd both said, nothing had happened.

After each successive round, the teams' decreasing scores grew closer and closer.

She and Adam had a chance to win, but she had to throw two 20s and a bull's-eye. It wasn't impossible, but she'd made a perfect score like that only twice in her life. The first time had been beginner's luck. The second time had been at a friend's bachelorette party with jumbo daiquiris in the mix and pictures of cute guys pinned to the board.

Chloe took her place behind the line. A hint of the jitters spread inside of her. She could do this. She *would* do it. Taking a long, cleansing breath, she shut out the room just like she did on set when she was absorbed in playing a part. This was a performance she had to nail, and instead of another actor, her costar was the board.

She threw the first dart and it hit the 20 mark. The second one did, too. Without overthinking it, Chloe threw the last dart. Bull's-eye.

"I did it!" She happy danced in place, then threw her arms around Adam who picked her up in a bear hug.

Mace smiled and toasted her with his beer while Tristan drank his.

Adam put her down. In a friendly gesture, he draped his arm around her shoulders as they joined Tristan and Mace at the table. "A winning throw like that deserves a celebration. Forget about wings. I'm buying you dinner."

"I agree," Mace said. "But you guys won so we're buying."

Chloe laughed. "I'm fine with just the wings."

"Are you kidding? We can't let that go uncelebrated." Adam dropped the score sheet on the table. "I'll put us on the reservation list. It's just the four of us, right?"

"Make it three." Tristan tossed a twenty on the table. "I'm going to finish watching the game, but I'll chip in for dinner." He looked to Chloe. "Have fun, Ace."

They'd all been having fun a few minutes ago. Why was he leaving? Chloe's enthusiasm dimmed.

After he left, Adam frowned. "What's wrong with him? He's never been a sore loser before."

Chloe stared at Tristan as he wove through the crowd, headed for the bar. "It's me."

Chapter Eleven

Tristan placed an order with the bartender. "I'll take a dozen Cajun wings to go. I also want to close out my tab."

Mace stepped up beside him. "Those better be the best wings on the planet."

"What are you talking about?"

"You're choosing them over steak, and what makes even less sense, you were rude to Chloe."

"I wasn't rude."

"She thinks you left because you don't like her."

The way Mace stared at him made Tristan feel like an ass. But he couldn't tell him that seeing her jump into Adam's arms without hesitation after their win had really gotten to him. He'd wanted to be the one holding her, and he'd even contemplated making it happen under the guise of giving her a congratulatory hug. How screwed-up was that?

The bartender handed Tristan his credit card and a computer tablet displaying his bill. He signed the screen and gave it back to her before turning to Mace. "I never told Chloe that I didn't like her."

"And you wouldn't because you actually do." Mace propped an elbow on the bar and faced him. "She's just not your usual type and that's throwing you off."

Sometimes, the instincts that made Mace a good deputy could make him a pain when it came to digging for the truth as a friend. "And what isn't my *usual* type?"

"Someone who prefers to live in the city and isn't into horses. In fact, when I first saw her, she kind of reminded me of—"

"Don't go there." Tristan held up his hand, cutting him off. He'd had that conversation with Rina. Hearing Erica's name mentioned twice in one week was too much, especially since he'd already established in his mind that there was no comparison between her and Chloe.

Tristan put his credit card in his wallet before stuffing the wallet into his back pocket. "Fine. I'll talk to her. Can you stay here and grab my take-out order?"

"Sure can, but you'll be saving it for tomorrow. You're joining us for dinner. They're seating us in twenty so make your apology good and quick."

Making amends and having dinner with them was probably the smart thing to do. Lingering tension wasn't a good thing with him, Adam and Chloe all working in the same space. "Where is she?"

"With Adam, waiting near the hostess station."

Tristan made his way through the crowd to the adjoining corridor connecting to the restaurant.

Chloe sat on one of the crowded black padded benches along the wall. She wouldn't look at him.

Adam, sitting beside her, gave him a hard stare and rested his shoulder on Chloe's as if in solidarity with her.

Tristan leaned down so she could hear him above the noise of conversations around them. "Can we step outside and talk a minute?" It looked as if she contemplated saying no. "Please?"

Chloe handed the restaurant beeper to Adam, then followed Tristan out a set of double doors near the end of the corridor.

Outside, couples and groups waiting for tables stood on a low-lit raised porch surrounded by a wood railing.

He and Chloe found a less populated spot in the far corner near the building and faced each other.

Tristan pushed out a breath. "I'm sorry for walking away like that after the game. Will you accept my apology?"

She crossed her arms over her chest. "Only if you tell me why you want me to fail."

"I don't."

"Well, you haven't exactly been cheering for me. All this week, when you weren't going out of your way to make sure to let me know you didn't want me around, you ignored me."

"No. You got it wrong. I wasn't ignoring you, I was busy, but you didn't seem to have a problem pushing your way into where you wanted to be."

"Pushing my way in?" Her brow rose. "If you would

have done what Zurie asked you to do in the first place, I wouldn't have had to resort to pushiness."

"I wasn't asked, I was told." An image of Gloria giving him an admonishing look reared up in his mind. "Look. I just wish Zurie would have consulted with me before deciding to have you tail me around. I would have been better prepared."

"Well, you weren't the only one affected. What about me? How do you think I felt when I found out she wasn't going to be here and I was stuck with you?"

Stuck with him? An objection made it to the tip of his tongue before he clamped his mouth shut. Yeah, that probably was a fair assessment. He'd been so caught up in his own problems, he really hadn't considered the circumstances from her perspective. "Okay, my apology is officially jacked up."

She gave him an exaggerated shocked look. "Amazing. We actually agree on something."

Tristan released a rueful chuckle. "I guess so." Tension he hadn't realized he'd been holding on to started to drain from him, and he rubbed over the prickling sensation at the back of his neck.

"Well, honestly, I can understand you wanting to be prepared." Chloe uncrossed her arms. "I don't like not knowing all the details about a situation either. I've only been a tad pushy because this audition is important to me, but I came up with a solution that solves both of our problems. Adam volunteered to help me with my research at the stable and to teach me about horses when he's off from work. You don't have to try and squeeze me into your schedule anymore."

Of course Adam volunteered. The urge to say no almost took precedence in Tristan's response. But Adam was giving them what they wanted, right? Chloe would learn what she needed to succeed with her audition, and he could focus on running the stable.

Still, Tristan considered the solution carefully. "Adam is good for the basics, but you should also spend time with Blake. As an experienced trainer, he'll have knowledge you'll want to tap into, as well. He can alternate with Adam in working with you during their shifts. Spending time with both of them will help you become more comfortable around the horses. Once you check that box, you'll be allowed to ride one."

"Allowed?" She laughed. "Let me guess. The reason you want them working with me during their shifts is so you can monitor me. You don't trust that I won't somehow pretend my way on a horse before you say I can ride one."

"No. Learning how to take care of a horse, first, is important. It's for your safety, that's all."

"Well, okay. Since you're putting it that way. It's nice to know that you actually care what happens to me, but you can relax. I'm not in a hurry to ride a horse, but I do need to learn more about them." Her smile contained a hint of teasing but also real happiness.

During the week, she'd shared a genuine smile with everyone but him. He'd just gotten his first, and he liked it…a lot. Tristan quelled the urge to lean in and capture that smile in a kiss as a personal victory. He opted for a handshake instead. "So do we have a deal?"

"I think it's more like a truce." Her smaller hand held his for an all-too-brief moment.

When she took her hand away, it was as if he could still feel the warmth and smoothness of her skin. He resisted taking her by the elbow to guide her back inside the restaurant. That seemingly harmless gesture would just make it harder not to keep touching her.

"Okay." He stepped back. "Sounds like we're good."

As they prepared to walk back to the restaurant, Chloe tried to ignore the nagging sensation that something was very much undone between her and Tristan. But what? They'd called a cease-fire and agreed to terms. She'd gotten all she wanted.

Still, for some reason, she had to force herself to smile. "I guess I'll let Adam know that we can skip tomorrow. It's his day off, and since we'll be working together now, I shouldn't take up his weekend."

"He'll appreciate it. I'll also let him and Blake know what we talked about so they can expect the additional duties in their schedule." Tristan glanced toward the restaurant entrance. "Then I guess we should go inside. They'll be calling our table soon." He turned to walk away.

Chloe grasped his arm. "Wait."

He stood patiently in front of her.

"There's something else we need to talk about."

His brow furrowed. "I'm listening."

What she was about to suggest was crazy, but at the same time it made sense. "We should kiss."

His brow sprang up. "We should what?"

"I'm only mentioning it because it keeps almost happening, but you have the stable to take care of. I have my audition. Almost kissing is a distraction we don't need." Tristan staring at her as if he wasn't sure he'd heard her right fueled a ramble. "If we kiss, we'll stop wondering and get over it. It'll be like checking it off a list. Done. Move on."

"So you think if we kiss, it'll be easier for us to do that?"

"Exactly. No more temptation. No more problems." He looked away from her as if mulling it over.

Seconds stretched, and Chloe was already prepared for his "no" answer.

"Let's do it." Tristan moved closer, and it took a moment for her to finally register he'd agreed.

"Okay." She laid her hands near his shoulders. Whoa, he was solid muscle, but that didn't matter. Getting this kiss out of the way was about not noticing him anymore. Should she leave her hands where they were or move them higher? Before she could decide what to do, he grasped her waist, brought her against him and covered her mouth with his.

Being close to all of that hard muscle and heat pulled out a breath that turned into a low moan. She slid her hands up and around his neck. His tongue drifted over hers, and the faint taste of hops flavored a deepening kiss that was equal parts goodness and sin. Chloe sank into him floating in a fathomless pool of wonderfulness as he coaxed, captivated and teased.

It was so good. She could stay there all night kissing him.

When it seemed he planned to ease away too soon, she grasped hold of his nape and pressed her lips more firmly to his and chased him for a longer kiss. Tristan caressed up and down her back, leaving heat and tingles behind as his hands came to settle low on her spine. His fingertips brushing just under the hem of her shirt made pleasure uncoil, and she lifted on her toes arching into him, yearning for more of his touch.

Voices and laughter filtered through a haze of heady desire.

He lifted his mouth a short distance away, and she remembered to breathe.

"So…" he murmured. "Did that clear things up?"

Tristan shifted his stance and widened his legs. Her curves locking in place against him like a piece in a puzzle raised so many impossible possibilities. She was there for only a few short weeks to learn all she could about the stable. Like they'd both agreed, being in each other's spheres raised too many distractions. She'd have to settle for that kiss.

The unconscious action of licking his lower lip tempted her to grab the front of his shirt and haul his mouth back down to hers. But she resisted, and eased away from him as she slid her arms from around his neck.

Tristan briefly tightened his hold on her waist but released her.

"You were right." He cleared his throat as he stepped back, putting even more space between them. "Now that we got that out of the way. We can move on to what's important."

Chapter Twelve

"*Move on...*"

That's what she was supposed to be doing. Chloe reminded herself of that for the umpteenth time as she stood outside the fenced-in arena where Blake rode Thunder Bay, a brown-and-white pinto that had been adopted by the stable a few months ago.

Five days had passed since Friday at the Montecito with Tristan, but she still couldn't forget what had happened on the porch. The strength of his arms as he held her close, the smell of his cologne filling her senses and the warmth of his mouth as he'd captured hers kept replaying in her mind. Usually at inopportune times when she was supposed to be paying attention and learning about the horses, like now.

But she was a professional. She knew how to separate her feelings from scripted actions. And they had scripted that kiss. It was planned out and wasn't some random, unexpected act.

Chloe spotted Tristan driving his black 4Runner down the road near the adjoining pasture to the stable parking lot. He'd left for a meeting someplace a little over three hours ago when she'd arrived at the stable at seven in the morning. Not that she was counting the hours in between seeing him or anything.

He hadn't lied about being busy. Tristan was in and out of his office all day, but he still kept his eye on the stable. He checked in with everyone regularly, but he wasn't a micromanager. He didn't have to be. His staff didn't hesitate in following through on his instructions or approaching him for advice. In fact, they went out of their way not to fall short on their duties and were comfortable with Tristan's high expectations of them.

"Whoa, Thunder." Blake commanding the horse pulled her focus back to the training session.

After the weekend, she'd spent the past Monday and Tuesday with Adam touring the stable and the pastures and learning the basics of the stable operation. Now she'd spend the next couple of days with Blake learning about the equipment or "tack" used in horse riding and about the care and training provided to the horses.

Some of the horses boarded in the stable and the pastures were fully taken care of by the staff from cleaning the stalls to feeding them to making sure they received proper care and exercise. Others were partially cared for by their owners who stopped by on a consistent basis. Five of the horses currently at the stable belonged to Tillbridge and Thunder was one of them.

According to Blake, Thunder's original owner hadn't properly trained him to follow basic commands but had used force. Thunder had learned not to trust having someone riding him and resisted having a bit in his mouth because he anticipated pain.

Blake had said when they'd first started working with him a few months ago, Thunder wouldn't respond to basic cues. Her lesson that morning had been about the slow, methodical retraining process they'd gone through with Thunder. He now responded to stopping just by voice command and had progressed to willingly accepting Blake's rein cues when they loped around the ring.

He dismounted Thunder. As he praised the horse, Blake rubbed him along the neck and shoulders. He looked to Chloe. "Any questions?"

She tossed her single braid, secured by one of Philippa's green bandanas, over her shoulder. Dressed similarly to him, her own Tillbridge pullover and jeans were dusty and rumpled, and she'd waded through enough crap that morning to consider her black tread-sole boots fully baptized. "No. That was interesting. Thunder is lucky to have found a home here."

"He's a good horse. With Tristan riding him, he'll become even better."

As Blake led Thunder from the arena to the stable, she stood a generous few feet away from both of them.

They walked past the spot where seeing the horses had frozen her in place before Tristan pulled her out of the way. But she was okay now with Thunder, right? Although they walked at a leisurely pace, she could feel her heart beating in her chest as her worst thoughts about horses started to take shape. What if Thunder got spooked by something, like a bird or a squirrel or just decided he wanted to run off? She didn't know what to do if Blake couldn't control him.

Stop! Thunder is good. Blake's good. I'm good. We're all good.

Chloe shifted her thoughts to the coolness of the midmorning that was quickly dissipating with the sun rising in an almost cloudless blue sky. She analyzed the dust and straw on her boots and the hem of her jeans and let her mind wander to what was becoming a continuing distraction. Tristan.

"So Thunder is Tristan's horse?" she asked.

"Yep. They're a good match. Tristan has plenty of patience."

Patience did seem to be one of Tristan's better qualities. He'd kissed her slow and easy the other night, as if he'd had all the time in the world.

They entered the stable.

Instead of straight down the middle aisle, he led Thunder to the right where the tack rooms and grooming stalls were located. "So are you getting excited about riding yet?"

Remembering not to get too close to Thunder's back end, she scooted forward next to Blake. "I can wait."

Blake laughed. "You look like I just asked you if you were ready for a root canal. It won't be that bad.

We'll put you on a gentle horse, probably Moonlight Joy. You'll be riding the trails in no time."

"What we've been doing for the past few days is fine. I actually don't have to ride a horse for my audition."

"But knowing how to care for a horse goes with knowing how to ride one. You can't not learn how to do both."

Oh, yes she could.

Another trainer walking by, a tall brunette with short hair outfitted in high black riding boots, tan breeches and a bright white pullover, stopped to ask Blake a few questions. As he answered, the woman followed him into the grooming stall where she helped cross tie Thunder and unbuckle the saddle.

Chloe moved out of the way as Blake took the saddle to the tack room beside the stall. The woman trailed behind him, asking his opinion about a company that sold riding gear.

The woman didn't work for Tillbridge, but she trained a few clients who boarded their horses there. Earlier, she'd been in the arena before them instructing a young girl who was riding a sleek black horse. When she'd asked him about the saddle the girl used, he'd said it was an English saddle. It was smaller, lighter and allowed the rider more contact with the horses. Something that was critical for events like show jumping.

In her opinion, it didn't look as sturdy as the larger, heavier Western saddle Blake had used on Thunder. The stirrups were also bigger and there was that horn part to hold on to. Not that it had helped her the last time she was on a horse.

But no worries about any of that. The character she hoped to play just worked at the stable. According to the notes that came with the script, she was more of a sidekick character that cheered the hero on and, of course, was secretly in love with him.

Even though the script didn't call for her to ride a horse, maybe she should at least sit on one with Blake or Adam holding on to it. She might feel comfortable doing that, but a trail ride—that was entirely unnecessary.

"She's a real gentle horse..."

That's what Blake had said about Moonlight Joy, but so had the last person she'd trusted to put her on a horse, and that one had made a run for it with her on its back.

But despite that bad memory, she'd done okay so far. On her first day with Adam, he'd had her feed the horses snacks as he introduced her to them.

She'd been terrified, but she'd pulled up her big-girl panties and handed out apple slices, carrots and hay cubes with a smile on the outside while screaming "get me out of here" on the inside.

Moonlight Joy actually had been the gentlest of all the horses as she'd eaten the apple slice from her hand. The only horse that hadn't been all that people friendly was Thunder. He'd given her massive stink eye and refused the treat. But she'd survived that immersion experience, hadn't she? In fact, she could even act out a moment like that on film if she had to and appear natural doing it.

The trainer gave Chloe a friendly smile as she

walked out of the tack room and went into the main part of the stable.

Blake came out and went to Chloe. "I'm going to the supply room to get some tail and mane detangler. We're going to groom Thunder first, and then we've got saddles to clean. While I'm gone, you can set up the grooming tools." He tipped his head toward where Thunder waited.

He was leaving her alone with the orneriest horse at the stable? Chloe backed up. "I don't mind getting the detangler. Third shelf down in the middle, right?"

"Right." He snagged her by the arm as she went to rush away. "But you already learned about feed and supplies when you were with Adam. Now it's time for you to move on to other things like grooming. Adam said he talked you through which tools to use in the right order. Let's see if you remember what he taught you. While I'm gone, you can set them up."

Long seconds later after Blake left, Chloe still stood outside the grooming stall.

Every neigh, whinny and clomp of horse hooves in the stable seemed magnified.

She willed herself not to run and forced herself to breathe. *Don't. Freak. Out.*

"You can do this," she whispered to herself. "Thunder is calm, and Blake is coming right back."

She took slow tentative steps into the stall with Thunder. "Hey there. It's me. Your good friend, Chloe."

Apparently, they were still on glaring terms because he just stood there, watching as she scooted to the narrow shelf attached to the sidewall with the tool caddy sitting on top of it.

She focused on the tools. "So. The way I see it, this whole grooming thing is like a mini spa moment for you. First, a manicure for your hooves. Or is it more like a pedicure?" As she picked up the hoof pick, she couldn't help but notice her own short, unpolished nails. An appointment with her manicurist was first on her agenda when she got home.

Chloe laid down the implement with a curved metal end and a brush. They'd use it to clear away any rocks or debris from Thunder's hooves. "What's next?"

Thunder fidgeted in place.

A slight frisson of unease moved down her spine. "You know, if you help me out, there could be an apple slice in your future."

Thunder shuffled closer to her. Prickles came over Chloe as if her skin and the stall were growing too small. "Okay." Her hands trembled slightly as she picked up one of the brushes. "I think this one is next."

Thunder shook his whole body from head to tail and snorted.

According to her translation of horse speak, that clearly meant he wanted her to leave. Message received.

Clutching the brush, Chloe rushed out just as heavy, booted footfalls approached the stall. Assuming it was Blake, she forced a breezy laugh. "Back already. I'm not done with my test."

"What test?" Tristan stood beside her instead of Blake.

Her heart flip-flopped harder and she almost threw

her arms around him. She could use a hug, but then he'd wonder what was wrong with her, and she'd have to explain. Not to mention, their kiss had sealed their unspoken hands-off agreement.

So act natural and don't make things weird. "Oh, I thought you were Adam. I mean Blake. I was with Adam yesterday, but you knew that." As she waved her hand from side to side emphasizing her point, she accidentally swatted the tip of her nose. "Insects, dust…it's everywhere, but you knew that, too." A random high-pitched laugh escaped. *Great.* She was an actress but she couldn't even act natural around him.

Tristan's gaze narrowed as he pointed at her face. "You have a scratch."

"Where?" Had she dinged herself in the nose? He probably saw her as not only awkward but clumsy. The ground just needed to open up and swallow her already.

He took her free hand that was still near her face and lowered it. As he peered down at the thin red welt on the back of it, he brushed his thumb over her knuckles.

Electric-like tingles spread from where he stroked near the scratch, careful to soothe and not cause her pain. She should have taken her hand from his, but the way he caressed her skin made her stand still for more.

Their gazes met and she barely breathed.

Tristan tightened his grasp on her and she drew air into her lungs. His wonderful scent wafted from the open V at the top of his button-down navy shirt that formed to his shoulders and chest. It drew her in and pulled her back. She definitely didn't smell or look as good as he did. His shirt and jeans where not only cleaned but neatly pressed, probably for the meeting he'd attended that morning.

She eased her hand from his. "It's nothing. I'm fine."

"You should still put antiseptic and a Band-Aid on it. If you're not careful, something as simple as this can easily turn into a problem."

"I'll do that after I finish my test."

"On what?"

"I'm supposed to line up the grooming tools we're going to use on Thunder. If I don't get it right, Blake will probably make me muck all of the stalls by myself."

"He's that hard-core, huh?"

"Absolutely. Apparently, he's got a tough boss looking over his shoulder, making sure I learn the proper way to do things."

Tristan glanced around, leaned in and spoke in a conspiratorial whisper. "If you want some help, I won't tell. If you don't."

The mischief in his eyes was a refreshing change from his usual seriousness and hard to resist without smiling at him. She handed him the brush. "My lips are sealed."

They crossed the threshold, and Tristan scratched Thunder's neck. "Hey, buddy."

"His Orneriness" morphed into sappy mush, whinnying softly as he butted Tristan's shoulder.

Seriously? Chloe stood behind Tristan and gave Thunder a long stare. *No apples for you, buddy.*

Tristan went to the shelf and she joined him, handing him the brush in her hand.

He took what she recognized as a currycomb from

the caddy. "I was actually looking for you. I wanted to ask you about this coming Saturday."

Saturday? Was he about to ask her out? No. Maybe he just wanted a dart game rematch. The possibilities along with her responses to them battled in her mind as she gave him her best passive but interested expression. "Oh? About what?"

"You're scheduled to shadow Adam this weekend, but Gloria just reminded me we have a kid's party scheduled at the stable this Saturday. You may want to sit this weekend out."

The kid's party. Of course he hadn't planned on asking her on a date. "I heard the staff talking about it. Actually, it sounds fun."

"Fun?" His brow raised. "You say that now, but when you're corralling hyper kids fueled by a massive sugar rush, you may wish you were mucking out stalls instead."

"It won't be that bad."

"You'd be surprised at the things they can get themselves into."

"I can handle it. Especially since there's going to be cake. Rina is making it along with a smaller one for the staff. Oh, but you wouldn't be interested that. It's chocolate not lemon."

"Sometimes, different is good." The low timbre of his voice prompted her to glance at him.

Was he talking about the cake?

Their shoulders brushed as she handed him the tools from the caddy and he arranged them. A small wave of giddiness hit. Had she moved closer, or had he?

"That's it." He gave her a slow, easy smile. "Add the sponges and cloths to the order and you're done, and don't forget. This is our little secret."

She crossed her heart.

He grinned as he headed out. "Oh, and use bananas."

"For what?"

He pointed to Thunder. "If you want to get on his good side, give him a few banana slices every now and then. He'll be your friend for life."

Blake walked into the stall carrying the bottle of detangler. He looked from Chloe to Tristan. "Hey, boss. Everything okay?"

"Everything is great." Tristan clapped Blake on the back. "Keep up the good work."

Blake gave him a nod. "Thanks."

The brunette trainer stopped Tristan just outside the stall to look over a paper.

Blake set the detangler next to the caddie. He smiled. "You did it right."

Chloe glanced at Tristan.

He winked at her. His grin was infectious.

Chloe smiled and winked back, but Blake caught her doing it. Faking annoyance, she blinked rapidly and swiped over her lashes, fighting not to laugh. "Crap, I got dust in my eye."

Chapter Thirteen

On Saturday, as Tristan walked up the wide dirt path from the stable, he briefly lifted the brim of his navy Tillbridge ball cap, and swiped sweat from his brow. Just like he'd predicted, the day was more hectic than usual with the general tasks of the stable plus the party.

Earlier that morning, the group, consisting of a dozen ten-year-olds had received a talk on horses and how they should conduct themselves around them. Afterward, the boys, who were on the same soccer team, had gone to the arena for mini riding lessons, taking their turns with Blake, another groom or a trainer leading each boy on a horse around the ring.

Up ahead, Chloe, who'd helped out with orientation and now with the lessons, collected black riding helmets and gloves from the last four riders and put them in nylon sacks.

She was doing surprisingly well around the horses. Honestly, he'd expected her to run from the task he'd had Adam assign her on her first day—give the horses treats—but she'd done it, and taken on every task so far despite her unease.

The other day, when he'd found her outside the grooming stall, she hadn't fooled him for a minute with her claim that she thought he was Blake coming to check on how she was doing with her test. He'd spotted the fear in her eyes. Admittedly, Thunder wasn't the friendliest horse, but she'd gotten past that and helped Blake groom him. The only thing she hadn't done, yet, was ride a horse. Maybe assisting at the party, and seeing the kids' eagerness to ride, might inspire her to want to get on one, too.

Near the entrance to the arena, Chloe traded fist bumps and high fives with the boys. "Good job."

One of the boys, head down, shoulders slumped, left her hanging. In an empathetic gesture, she patted his shoulder.

"Okay, guys." Blake called out. "Remember what we said about making sure you stay hydrated? Head over to the van for cold drinks and a pit stop."

Most of the boys raced down the path toward Tristan. Two of the fathers, acting as chaperones, rounded up stragglers. The dejected boy lingered around a man preoccupied with talking on his cell who had the same close-cut dark hair and naturally light tan skin. Lean and already taller than most of the other boys, he'd most likely reach his father's height, possibly even exceed it.

They walked past, and it took a second for Tristan to make the connection that the man was the one who'd stopped by the office three weeks ago and signed the party contract with Gloria. His name was Sam Harrold and his son, the boy whose birthday was being celebrated, was E.J. But from the sad look in E.J.'s eyes, it wasn't much of a celebration for him. All he wanted was his father's attention.

"Hey, Tristan."

Chloe waved at him and his heart thumped. Meeting with Philippa at the guesthouse was next on his schedule, but ever since his kiss with Chloe, the push and pull that he'd felt around her from the start had heightened to a distinct pull. Just knowing she was around made him want to see her. Hell, he'd even found himself coming up with multiple excuses to find her but had rationed his contact with her to once a day. But it wasn't enough. Just like the kiss they'd shared.

That night at the restaurant, when she'd mentioned it, he'd half heard her claims about moving on and getting it out of the way. His own reasoning about it didn't come with any justifications. He'd just wanted to kiss her. Afterward, he'd said he was all good, but the warmth of her mouth, the way she'd tasted of lime from her drink and had fit so perfectly against him, had taken up permanent residence in his mind.

As he met Chloe partway down the path, Blake, leading the horses back to the stable with the trainer, gave him a nod. Curiosity also passed through his expression as he briefly glanced from Tristan to Chloe.

Tristan brushed it aside. Checking in with her was part of the management responsibilities Zurie had assigned him.

Chloe smiled at him. With her hair pulled back in a braid, and her face devoid of makeup, she had a natural glow. "You missed the fun."

"I did, huh?" The urge to take her hand was strong, but he took one of the bags from her instead. "How's the party going?"

"Good, I think. No bruises, blood or missing children."

"Yet. You still have time to sneak out?"

"And miss the hayride to the pasture and the cookout?"

"Don't you mean the cake?"

She laughed. "Yeah that, too, but honestly, I can't help but smile watching this group enjoying themselves."

Using her hand to shade her eyes from the late-morning sun, she peered to the right at the boys now in the seating area a short distance from the stable.

"You don't have a hat?"

"Gloria gave me one, but I forgot it."

It felt more than right to offer her his. He took it off but paused before setting it on her head. What if she didn't want to wear it?

Chloe set down the bag and took the hat from his hands. "Thanks. You're a lifesaver. Are you sure you don't mind?"

A hint of pride swelled in his chest as she put it on. It looked better on her than it did on him. "Not at all."

Animated voices and cheers came from the group.

She picked up the bag from the ground and slipped the other one from his hand. "I need to put these away before we leave. I scored a front seat in the tractor on the way to the hayride. I don't want to lose my spot. Sure you don't want to tag along for the cookout?"

"I can't. I have a meeting with Philippa to finalize plans for the Spring Fling. After that, I'm heading to Baltimore to have dinner with a friend."

"Oh." Her smile dimmed a little. "That sounds fun."

"Yeah, it will be. I haven't seen him in a while." For some reason he felt the need to explain more. He wasn't going on a date. "He was a pro bull rider. He wants to talk about a horse he's planning to sell."

"That sounds nice." Her wide smile returned. "The Spring Fling, it's this coming Wednesday, isn't it? I'm glad you said that. When Rina dropped off the cake earlier, she told me to call her today or tomorrow. Something about party favors? Do you know what that means?"

"No idea, but knowing her, it involves cocktails."

"Ooh, I like the sound of that."

Rina wanting to get to know Chloe better on a personal level meant Rina liked her. She didn't hang out with people she didn't. "I won't hold you up then. You can give me the hat back later."

"Maybe." As Chloe walked away with the bags,

she gave him a playful smile as she adjusted the visor. "I kinda like how it fits."

He did too.

Chapter Fourteen

Chloe waved goodbye to the group from the parking lot at the stable as the boys and their fathers drove away in two SUVs on the adjacent road. After a hayride to an area near a vacant pasture for burgers, hot dogs, cake and games, the party had come to an end.

E.J. waited in the front passenger seat of a black four-door luxury car parked in the lot while his father, talking on his cell, stood nearby. She didn't have to see the boy's face to know he had a sullen expression. He'd worn it the entire day.

She'd heard they were staying at the guesthouse this weekend. Hopefully, his dad would finish whatever had kept him busy during the birthday party so he could devote more time to his son.

Blake waited for her at the edge of the lot near the

path leading to the stable. "You look like you're ready to fall over."

"I ran out of energy somewhere between the water bucket race and the impromptu soccer game."

"Same here. Why don't you take off? I can handle the rest."

"Are you sure?" Even as she asked, she couldn't stop her shoulders from slumping in relief.

"Yeah. Me and one of the other grooms will pick up the rest of the equipment at the pavilion in the morning. I'm just going to check the stall one more time, then I'm out."

Ten minutes later, she trudged into the guesthouse tired and hungry. It was only four in the afternoon, and the sun hadn't gone down yet, but she was definitely in for the rest of the day.

After a semilong hot shower, she got comfy in an off-the-shoulder gray sweatshirt and peach yoga pants, then collapsed on the bed. She should review the horse stable terms she'd written down on the pad sitting on the dresser, along with the horse encyclopedia, anatomy chart and horse care books Blake had loaned her. Some might consider studying all of that overkill, but the more she understood, the less chance she'd be caught off guard during her audition.

Her gaze drifted to Tristan's hat on the crimson chair by the window, and a smile, as big as the one that had taken over her face when he'd loaned it her, took over her face. She'd behaved like a schoolgirl with a crush, practically snatching the hat from his hand, but it had felt so good to wear it. And it gave her a reason to see him again. Maybe she'd buy him lunch as a thank-you and drool over him in the process.

Most of the guys she'd gone out with back in California sculpted their bodies in a gym for show. But Tristan's strength was honed from handling horses, lifting feed bags and carrying around supplies. He wasn't too good or too busy to jump in and help out if needed, and the staff seemed to appreciate that about him.

Just like she appreciated the way he filled out a T-shirt and a pair of jeans. He probably looked even sexier wearing a cowboy hat.

Commotion in the hallway pulled her from daydreaming. Someone was yelling as if they were upset, and the voice sounded familiar.

She got up and peeked outside the door

E.J.'s father stood at the end of the hallway with Philippa. "I don't care if you have to search every room in this place."

"We're doing that now, Mr. Harrold." Philippa pointed to members of the Tillbridge staff at the other end of the hall, knocking on doors. "We're talking to all the guests, and someone is searching the stable. I've also contacted the local sheriff's department as a precaution."

"The sheriff's office…" His shoulders drooped and his head fell forward. "E.J. can't be lost. We have to find him."

E.J. was missing? Concern drove Chloe back inside where she hurriedly changed into a T-shirt and jeans. After shoving her feet into a pair of tennis shoes, she grabbed her key card, and ran out the door.

Downstairs near the front desk was a buzz of activity.

Philippa directed members of the housekeeping staff to search the area around the cottages.

Curious and concerned guests questioned the front desk clerk about what was going on. Some of them even offered to help with the search.

E.J.'s father stood talking to Mace in the seating area. He swiped impatiently over the screen of his phone. "I have pictures of him. I know I do."

The other fathers at the party had taken pictures of the boys and E.J. riding horses and at the cookout. If he couldn't find one, he could contact them, but she'd give him a minute to find one before making that suggestion.

Philippa's gaze locked with hers, and Chloe went to her. "What can I do to help?"

Just as Philippa was about to answer, Tristan came through the door.

He glanced at Mace with E.J.'s father, then went straight to Philippa who looked surprised to see him.

"I thought you were going to Baltimore," she said.

"I was only a few miles away from here when Blake called. Any new information on the boy?" Clean-shaven, and dressed in jeans and a long-sleeved white pullover with the sleeves pushed up, he smelled appealingly of cologne, just like he had the night they'd played darts.

"No." Philippa shook her head. "We're still talking to guests and checking the cottages."

"When was the last time his father saw him?" he asked.

"A little over a half hour ago in the restaurant at dinner." Philippa's gaze went to E.J.'s father. "He got a phone call and was having problems hearing the person on the line, so he left E.J. at the table and went to the hallway just past the hostess station. When he came back, E.J. was gone."

Worry ticked up in Chloe. "Did anyone in the restaurant notice E.J. leaving?"

"No one we've spoken to, so far, but it was busy when he and his father were there. Most people were focused on the menu or their meals, and not everyone who was dining in the restaurant is staying here at the guesthouse. Some of them have already left."

The weighted pause in the conversation allowed room for unsettling speculation. Had E.J. left on his own or been taken by a stranger? The possibility brought up a sick feeling in Chloe. Unconsciously, she'd moved closer to Tristan, and she welcomed the solid press of his arm against hers.

"What about the security cameras?" he asked. "The one in the hall outside of the restaurant entrance could have caught him walking out."

"That's what I thought, too, but apparently it wasn't in a good position to get a clear view." Chloe and Tristan followed Philippa's glance toward the open door to an office behind the reception desk. "One of the sheriff's deputies is scanning the footage from the other cameras for clues."

"Do you know what he was wearing?" Tristan asked.

"Jeans, a yellow T-shirt with red lettering on it and mostly white tennis shoes." Philippa's phone buzzed, and a trace of uncertainty came into her face. She looked to Tristan. "It's Zurie. I was on the phone with her at the front desk when Mr. Harrold alerted us that E.J. was missing. She's probably calling to find out what happened. Do you want to talk to her?"

"No. You give her an update. I'm heading to the stable to pick up a radio and check in with Blake, then I'm going to look for E.J. Someone needs to contact me with any new details from the deputies about the search so we can coordinate with them."

"I'll tell Mace."

"I'm coming with you," Chloe interjected. "I mean, unless you're riding horses to do it."

"No. I'm driving." His gaze moved down and up. "A storm's coming in. Do you have a rain jacket?"

"I don't."

"I've got an extra one. Come on." He led the way out of the guesthouse.

Gray clouds obscured the late-evening sun, and thunder rumbled in the distance.

Once they buckled into their seats in his 4Runner, he sped out of the parking lot and hung a left on the main road.

The open grassy field belonging to Tillbridge was on the left. Another field dotted with trees endlessly unfolded on the other side of the road.

He made two more lefts and stopped in the stable

parking lot. "I'll be right back." He jumped out and jogged to the back door of the stable leading to the hallway outside of his office.

Moments later, he came back out wearing a short dark green rain jacket and carrying another matching jacket and a two-way radio.

She accepted both as he got back in the SUV. "Still no signs of E.J.?"

"Not in the stable or fields near the guesthouse. Blake's taking an ATV to check the riding trails. We're driving to the north and south pastures."

Rain started to fall intermittently. Each plop on the windshield marked time, magnifying the seconds passing without hearing good news.

The radio crackled. *"Tristan—this is Mace."*

She handed it to him and he pressed the talk button. "Go ahead, Mace."

"We just finished reviewing the security footage. The boy slipped out alone from the side entrance facing the cottages. Over."

"If he made it past the cottages, he could be in the south pasture. We're heading that way now."

"Copy that. We'll widen our search in the other directions. Keep me posted on this channel."

"Roger, out."

Chloe accepted the radio back. "The south pasture—that's near the area where we held the cookout. Do you think he made it that far?"

Tristan drove out of the parking lot and turned onto the road. "At this point, we can't rule anything out. I'm just wondering what he was thinking when he left his dad. Did he just wander off because he was bored or was he planning to run away?"

"Or was he upset over being ignored? His father stayed on his phone for almost the entire party. He barely acknowledged E.J. during the riding lessons. In fact, I don't think he took one picture of E.J. or the party."

"I noticed his dad checking out, too. The same thing happening at dinner had to have really hurt him." Tristan released a heavy breath. "Some parents just don't understand that nothing else can make up for them being there when their kids need them."

Chloe couldn't imagine otherwise. Growing up, her mom and dad had been overachievers in the paying attention department. They'd never missed a dance recital, school play or game where she'd been a cheer-leader. Her junior year of high school, she'd complained to them about needing more independence, aka time with her captain of the football team boyfriend. They'd reluctantly agreed to keep their distance.

Tristan pulled up to the closed pasture gate, and she started pulling on the jacket he'd given her. "I'll open it."

After he told her the code to the locking mecha-nism, she flipped up the hood of the jacket and got out.

The wind molded the oversized jacket to her and whipped the hem around the top of her thighs as she hurried to unlock the gate. She waited for him to drive in, closed it, then hopped back in the car.

Her shivers caught Tristan's attention, and he turned off the cool air blowing through the vents. As he drove the perimeter, they came upon a smaller gated area on the right where the cookout had been held.

Tristan parked. "Stay here, I'll check around." He got out and entered the gated area.

The grill that had been set up under the pavilion was gone, replaced by the folded white tents, chairs and buffet tables on the concrete slab.

He walked past it to the corner bar used for adult parties that was covered by a tarp. He briefly looked under the covering, then walked around to the other side.

Was E.J. under there?

Tristan bent down.

Hope dissipated when he stood with just a soccer ball in his hand.

He jogged to the car and tossed the ball in the back seat as he got in. "I'm guessing this belongs to E.J."

"Or one of his friends. They were kicking a couple of them around during the cookout."

The rumble of thunder reverberated through her seat. Suddenly it was if every cloud in the sky had opened up and rained poured out of them.

"Oh, no. He'll get soaked." Helplessness intertwined with her concern. Was E.J. scared? Hopefully, he'd be as brave as he'd been when he'd gotten on a horse for the first time that afternoon.

Tristan reached over and squeezed her hand.

She squeezed back, appreciating they weren't trading baseless reassurances that E.J. would just turn up. She, Tristan and everyone else had to do their best to find him.

He started the SUV. "There's one more place we need to search while we're here."

"Where? It's just an open field."

"The run-in." Tristan pointed to the open wood shelter on the far side of the field barely visible in the rain.

Chapter Fifteen

As Tristan drove across the grassy field, Chloe peered through the rain flooding the windshield and battled disappointment. She didn't see anything near the run-in. "Where do we go from here?" she asked.

"We'll head north."

As the windshield wiper in front of her swept past clearing away the rain, she spotted a small patch of yellow in the corner of the open structure with a low sloped roof. Philippa had said E.J.'s shirt was that color. "I see something!"

"Where?"

She pointed, hoping it wasn't an illusion. "There… near the end on the left. See it?"

"I do." Tristan sped up, and the patch of yellow took form.

"It's him!"

Once he stopped the car, they both jumped out.

E.J. sat against the back of the partial enclosure, his thin arms wrapped around his knees that were pulled up to his chest. He looked up at them. Hints of apprehension filled his face along with relief, as if he expected to be scolded.

Tristan took off his jacket and hunkered down in front of him. "Hey, little man. You okay?"

Shivering, E.J. snuggled into the jacket Tristan laid over him. "I hurt my ankle when I tripped."

"Which one?" Chloe knelt beside him. Lifting the hem of the jacket around his legs, she revealed his dirt-smudged sneakers.

E.J. wiggled his right foot and winced.

Tristan grasped his shoulder. "Can I take a closer look?"

He nodded and Tristan took off E.J.'s shoe. "It's definitely swollen. You might have sprained it. I'll carry you to the SUV. Then I'll radio in to let your dad know that you're okay."

E.J. shrank away and blinked back tears. "Dad doesn't care, he's just mad at me."

"No." She and Tristan spoke at the same time.

From the stiff set of E.J.'s little shoulders, he didn't want anyone to coddle him. Chloe patted his knee instead. "Your dad is really worried about you."

"All he cares about is work." Tears welled in E.J.'s eyes. "I wish we never came here. I didn't want a stupid party." His voice cracked. "I just wanted to be with my dad." He dipped his head and started to cry.

Scooting closer, Chloe drew him into a hug and E.J. held her tight. Nothing in the hundreds of scripts she'd read in the past could help her find the words to comfort him. She swallowed against a lump in her throat. With all the effort his dad had put into the party, surely he loved him. E.J. shivered helplessly against her, and Chloe started to choke up even more as she held him a bit tighter.

Tristan bent down. He soothingly stroked her back as he whispered in her ear. "I'll be right back."

He went to the SUV and returned a moment later with the radio. "Mace wants us to sit tight. Your dad is coming with him." He crouched down eye level with E.J. "And he wants to talk to you."

E.J. wiped his eyes. "He does?"

Tristan handed him the radio. "Push this button on the side so he can hear you."

E.J. pressed the button. "Dad?"

"E.J.—is that you? I'm coming. It's okay. I'll be there in less than a minute."

"Dad… I'm sorry. I left my ball behind…the nice one you gave me last Christmas. I just wanted to find it."

"I know. I should have let you know that I heard you when you told me that at dinner."

The squawk from a siren drew their attention. A patrol car with flashing blue lights cut across the pasture.

As soon as it stopped, E.J.'s dad got out of the front passenger seat and hurried over to them.

Tristan stood to the side, out of his way, and helped Chloe to her feet. Pinpricks raced over her legs from kneeling in an awkward position. She leaned on him and he wrapped an arm around her waist.

As Mr. Harrold hugged E.J. his eyes closed as if he was saying a silent prayer.

"Dad, I'm sorry." E.J. burrowed into his father's chest. "I got scared."

"It's okay. I'm here now." E.J.'s father scooped him up in his arms.

Seeing father and son holding each other as E.J.'s dad carried him to the patrol car filled Chloe's chest with soft emotions. They clearly had some kind of bond. Hopefully, E.J. would find a way to tell his father what he told her and his father would listen.

Mace gave Chloe and Tristan a nod. "Good job on finding him. There's an ambulance on its way to the guesthouse. I'll see you there." He hustled to his patrol car.

Suddenly, Tristan released her. "The soccer ball." He hurried to the SUV, took it from the back seat, and handed what had led to the evening's adventure to E.J. who sat in the back cuddled next to his dad.

They returned Tristan's jacket.

Mace drove off with them.

Tristan came back to her. He slipped his jacket back on. "E.J.'s dad said to tell you thank you."

The exhale that rushed out of her, as if she'd been holding her breath the entire time while looking for E.J., came with unexpected tears. She fanned her face. "Why am I crying? We found him. It's over."

Tristan tugged her by the hand, pulling her closer, then held her by the waist. "It's been a rough hour."

"It really has." Needing more contact with him, she rested her forehead against his shoulder, not caring that he was wet from the rain. "I was afraid that we wouldn't find him."

"But we did." He slid his hands farther around her and stroked up and down her back.

The soothing glide of his touch lured her into slipping her arms into his jacket and wrapping them around his waist. His shirt had gotten wet during the short time E.J. had had his jacket but he was still toasty warm.

As they breathed in sync, awareness built of how her breasts were pillowed against his chest. She could feel the tautness of his stomach, and her hips where aligned with his.

Was she the only one who felt it?

She eased back to look at him, and what she saw in his eyes confirmed he did, too. His palms gliding to her back and his slow lean in made her heart skip beats. Tristan's lips touched hers and each coaxing brush of his mouth left Chloe suspended in anticipation for the next one. As his tongue swept over her lower lip, she opened up to him on a sigh.

Where their kiss at the restaurant raised more curiosity and "what if" questions, this one clarified exactly what existed between them. Undeniable desire as strong as the thunder shaking the ground underneath her feet. It dismantled the foundation of reason and obliterated warnings about obligations and responsibilities, and why she should be concerned about them.

Tristan pulled her flush against him and Chloe slipped both of her arms around his neck, losing herself in the slow, decadent, bone-melting heat unfurling inside of her as Tristan teased, explored and laid claim to every curve and hollow of her mouth. She sank impossibly deeper into him.

As he swept kisses near her ear, his unsteady exhale tingled over her cheek. "Chloe?"

He didn't need to say more. The tone of his voice said everything. Tristan wanted her and needed to know if she wanted him just as much.

"Yes." As he kissed her neck, she tilted her head, giving him better access. "But can we get out of the rain?"

"Yeah, definitely." He pressed a lingering kiss to her lips. "Let's go."

She flipped up the hood of her jacket. Tristan took her hand and intertwined his fingers with hers, as they rushed to the SUV. He let go of her and she went to the front passenger door and he went to the driver's side. Their eyes met before they got in, and what she saw in his face made her heart beat faster. And conveyed what was in her own thinking. She didn't want to wait.

Without a second guess, she opened the back door of the SUV and he did the same on the driver's side. She scrambled into the back seat with him, and as soon as the doors shut, Chloe willingly went into his arms. But their heated kisses weren't enough. Despite the cramped space, she started to crawl onto his lap, but his grasp on her hips prevented it.

"Hold on." Tristan reached around and tossed his phone in the driver's seat. Then he pulled the side lever on it.

The seat fell forward, giving them a little more room.

Tristan's phone buzzed with a message, but he ignored it.

Chloe straddled him, and in between all too brief kisses he unzipped her jacket, and she shrugged it off. Eager for the chance to run her hands over what she'd been dreaming about ever since that day at his cottage—his impressive chest and abs—she helped him take off his and reached for the hem of his pullover.

But Tristan's deepening kiss, and his hand skimming underneath the front of her shirt and rising to cup her lace-covered breast distracted her. He flicked his thumb over her nipple and Chloe's breath hitched. He kept stroking over the peak and desire spiraled down to her middle.

His phone buzzing several times and chiming with an incoming call made them both pause and look in that direction.

Everyone was probably wondering where they were. The realization cooled Chloe's desire. "You should probably get that. Mace did say he'd see us at the guesthouse."

Tristan slipped his hand from underneath her shirt. "Yeah, he did." He laid his forehead briefly to hers. "And knowing him, he'll come looking for us or send another deputy." His phone chimed again with an incoming call, and he released a long exhale. "Can you reach my phone?"

She crawled off his lap, leaned between the seats and snagged the phone.

He accepted it from her and looked at the screen "It's Philippa."

As Tristan answered, Chloe righted her clothes, and slipped her jacket back on.

Wow. She'd rocketed from zero to the back seat of his car, tearing at his clothes in no time flat. She hadn't been turned on by a guy enough to become that impulsive since when? College?

"Okay. I'm on my way back to the guesthouse now," Tristan said to Philippa over the phone. "We'll talk more about it when I get there." He ended the call.

"Everything okay?"

"Yes. Everyone is relieved that E.J. is safe. Philippa and Mace want to talk about the security camera issue." He paused and silence sat between them. "Chloe, I…"

Thunder boomed and shook the ground. Rain poured over the windshield.

His mouth flattened with a concerned expression. "We should go before it gets worse."

She hopped out seconds before him, and by the time Chloe got into the front she was soaked and so was Tristan.

He swiped water from his face and blinked it from his eyes, then started the engine. His phone rang and he connected it to the SUV's Bluetooth system before he answered. This time it was Blake—a part of the path leading from the stable to the arena was flooded because it wasn't draining properly. Unfortunately, they couldn't address it now. They'd have to wait until the rain let up, probably in the morning.

Tristan ended the call as they drove into the guesthouse parking lot. He pulled into a spot near the front entrance. "You ready to make a run for it?"

"I'm ready."

They jumped out at the same time.

On the way to the steps, as she leaped over a puddle, Tristan caught her by the hand. He didn't let go until they reached the steps to the covered porch where Mace waited for them.

Unlike at the bar, Mace was all business when he gave her a nod. "Thanks again for helping out, Chloe." He turned to Tristan. "Got a minute?"

And just like that, her moment with Tristan was over. Stolen by responsibility…and a confusing reality. Avoiding distractions wasn't the only reason she shouldn't get involved with Tristan. She was really attracted to him, but was temporarily living another life. How many times in her career had she witnessed actor's getting involved with someone living in the place where they were filming, only to have regrets or hurt feelings because things got unexpectedly complicated.

During the time she had left at Tillbridge, she didn't need complicated, right?

Chapter Sixteen

Chloe sipped the spritzer in her wineglass. The refreshing mix of grapefruit soda and rosé flowed down smoothly…maybe a bit too smoothly. She set the glass next to her plate on the yellow-striped place mat. "These cocktails are dangerous."

"Tell me about it." Philippa sat next to her at the oval wood table in Rina's dining room. She set down her own half-full glass. "The strawberry vodka in this one really gives it a kick. Too many of these, and I'll be camped out on your couch for the night."

Rina, sitting across from them, smiled. "I'll take that as a yes for adding these to the Sunday brunch menu at Brewed Haven. What about the rest of it?" She pointed to the dishes of food on the table.

"My vote is yes for all of this, too." Chloe spooned

a little more of the baked blueberry French toast, and the spinach, mushroom and artichoke quiche on her plate. "I appreciate the invite."

She'd needed the distraction. Otherwise, she may have sat in her room thinking about Tristan and wondering what he thought about their kiss the day before. Would things now be awkward between them at the stable? Should they talk about what happened?

As Philippa added the same foods to her plate along with a mini iced muffin, she looked to Chloe. "You do realize her making us Sunday brunch is actually a bribe to get us to help her with the Spring Fling gift bags. She's hoping we'll be too full and tipsy to notice that she's making us work on our day off."

"Not true." Rina laughed as she flipped her braids over her shoulder. "Okay, yes, I am going to put you to work, but it's not a bribe just a thank-you beforehand."

"Uh-huh." Philippa gave Rina a knowing smirk. "But it's an even trade on my end. I'm stealing a couple of these ideas for Pasture Lane."

The two besties started bantering over recipes and menu ideas.

Absorbed in the delicious flavors of savory, salty and sweet, Chloe sat back and listened. Like them, she was relaxed and comfortable in a T-shirt and jeans, content to eat good food and hang out with them in Rina's two-bedroom apartment above the Brewed Haven Café.

The large windows overlooking Main Street in the town and covering most of the far wall from the dining room to the adjoining living room let in lots of sunlight.

Soft white walls along with dark wood furniture, and a cream, tangerine and turquoise color palette, gave the space a light, airy welcoming feel.

Rina and Philippa's almost nonstop conversation moved from recipes to the cute new guy that had started delivering vegetables to the restaurant and the café that looked like one of the actors on a Netflix series they were both binge watching—No. Chloe didn't know the actor personally—to how Rina had the best commute time ever to the café from her recently renovated apartment.

They finished eating and Chloe pitched in with clearing the dishes to the adjoining kitchen. After that, they went to the living room.

"So ladies, here it is. Fifty of everything." Rina set her full wineglass on the large square coffee table, then spread her hands over the stacks of medium-sized folded navy-and-white gift bags, photos, flash drives, wine openers, chocolate, merchant coupons and other small items grouped on the table and floor. "I think we should start with putting the photos in the albums first."

Chloe sat down with a glass of water on the opposite side of the table on the cream couch. "Sounds good to me."

Philippa dropped down next her, wine spritzer in hand. "So what's on the flash drive?"

"More pictures of the Tillbridge staff from the past year." Rina eased down to the natural beige rug. Philippa tossed her a turquoise pillow from the couch. Rina stretched out her right leg and stuck the pillow under her knee. "Almost everyone complained last year about not getting the usual keepsake album we normally give so this year we're doing both."

Philippa picked up one of the blue four-by-six-inch albums. She raised a brow. "Well, now we know where the money for my prime rib went."

"But we're still having it." Rina flashed her an overly bright smile. "I never doubted you."

"Yeah, yeah, you can stop with the pep talk." Philippa waved a hand playfully dismissing her. "Lucky for everyone, I did manage it, barely. Speaking of managing things. How's the horse riding going, Chloe? Your first time must have been a thrill."

"Well...that hasn't happened yet, and it's not necessary." Philippa's and Rina's puzzled stares required her to give an explanation. "I really just need to know more about horses and be comfortable around them for my audition."

Rina shook her head. "I don't see how you can truly be comfortable around them without riding one. What did Tristan say? I'm surprised he's not all over you."

An image of her and Tristan in his SUV popped into Chloe's mind. She took a needed sip of cool water.

"Well, I'm not," Philippa added. "Tristan's time is spread thin with running the entire place. I don't think he's had a day off. When I called my supervisors this morning, they said he and Mace were checking the security cameras again because of what happened yesterday."

Over brunch, the three of them had talked about E.J. running away.

"They also said Zurie was calling around looking for him," Philippa added. "Apparently, he isn't answering his phone."

From the knowing looks Rina and Philippa exchanged this wasn't an unexpected occurrence. "He'll call her back when he has something new to tell her."

Philippa chuckled. "I guess. It's still amazing to me that those two are so far apart now. They were rodeo twins at one time."

Chloe almost choked on a sip of water. "Twins— Zurie and Tristan?"

Rina hauled herself up from the floor. "You don't believe it? I have proof." She walked down the hall behind her.

Philippa looked to Chloe. "I hope you're ready for this because she's coming back with at least two huge books of photos." She chuckled and settled back on the couch with her drink. "And she claims it's everyone else who wants the photo albums at Spring Fling. Right."

True to Philippa's prediction, Rina returned with the two albums as well as a scrapbook.

After making space on the coffee table for them, Rina wedged herself between Chloe and Philippa and cracked open the first album. "Their twinsie moments when she was ten and he was four. That's when Zurie started actively competing in rodeos and he idolized her. Here they are at one of her events."

In the photo, a cute precocious-looking Tristan and smiling pint-size Zurie were geared up in cowboy hats, button-downs, jeans and cowboy boots. They had an arm wrapped around each other as she held up a blue ribbon with a medallion in her free hand.

The series of photos that followed on the pages showed them both growing older, Tristan becoming taller than Zurie, both holding trophies and ribbons and still smiling at each other like best buds.

"What events did they compete in?" Chloe asked. "And where were you?"

"Zurie's main event was barrel racing. Tristan started out with calf riding, then moved up to riding bulls. They both competed in rodeos through high school. Me? I lived and breathed show jumping."

Rina flipped the page and pointed to one of the photos of her as a teen, smiling next to a dark horse. A small sad smile came over her face as she stroked the edge of the photo of her younger self dressed in the traditional English riding style with high boots, tan breeches, a short black jacket and a riding helmet.

Sometimes, Rina walked with a slight limp. Did she injure herself during a competition?

Rina turned the page again to several photos. She pointed out her mother, her father, Mathew, and Tristan's father, Jacob. The two men, twins, resembled Tristan in their height and build and had Rina and Zurie's dark brown skin tones. The two sisters looked like their mother.

"And here's one of all of us in front of our family home at Christmas. It was where the guesthouse is now."

Where was Tristan's mom? In the pictures of him when he was younger, it was Zurie and Rina's mom who doted over him. Chloe had so many questions, but her new, growing friendship with Rina outweighed curiosity.

Philippa tapped the photo of the Tillbridges, bundled up in winter clothing on a snowy day, smiling for the camera. Behind them, Christmas lights were strung along the roof of the house and a wreath with a red bow hung on the door.

"That place was more like a mini mansion. All those bedrooms, a huge family room and that kitchen." Philippa moaned. "It was a cook's dream with an eight-burner stove, a center island, a huge refrigerator and a walk-in pantry. And your mama owned that space like a boss."

"Yes, she did." Rina laughed. "It wasn't quite a mansion, but it was large enough for all of us to live there comfortably."

"It looks like you had fun together," Chloe said.

"We did." Rina's voice grew softer. "I really miss those days."

Philippa gave her a friendly nudge. "Keep turning the pages."

More photos of Rina's, Zurie's and Tristan's lives were revealed.

Philippa peered at ones of Tristan and Zurie in various rodeos. "Those two were so obsessed. I'm surprised they stopped competing altogether."

"Yeah, especially since they were so good." Rina pointed to a corner photo. "Here she is in one of her last barrel racing competitions."

Zurie looked to be at least twenty. The expression

under her white cowboy hat was all business as she adjusted the saddle on a tan horse. The remaining photos showed her racing the horse around what looked like red, white and blue metal storage drums in a large arena.

"What age did Tristan stop competing?" Chloe asked.

"Around the same age Zurie did, when he was twenty. He joined the army. But he was hardheaded enough to start up again for a short time when he got out four years ago."

Rina shifted the book on her lap closer to Chloe, and a photo slipped out the back of the album to the floor.

Chloe picked it up. The picture appeared to be a more recent photo of Jacob in a black tux. He was fifty-ish, maybe? He was cutting into a four-tiered wedding cake with a much younger woman wearing a form-fitting wedding gown.

"Oh." Rina reared back a little. "How did that get in there?"

"Who is she?" Chloe handed her the photo.

Rina tucked it away between pages at the end of the album. "That's Jacob's wife, Erica."

Philippa huffed a breath. "Otherwise known as the gold digger."

Chloe couldn't see Rina's face as she cocked her head and stared at Philippa, but Philippa's "whatever" expression, along with Rina's reaction to the photo a minute ago, filled in the gaps about Tristan's young stepmom.

She wasn't very popular.

"Anyway." Rina turned back to Chloe. "This is what I wanted to show you."

She turned the pages of the album and pointed to photos of Tristan in motion, riding a bull. Another showed him more recently, looking larger than life, walking alone through what looked like a stadium tunnel in full riding gear from boots to chaps to black protective vest and a black cowboy hat.

Chloe's heart ticked up a beat. Suddenly warm from the inside out, she picked up her glass and took a long drink. Strange. Cowboys had never been her usual type.

Tristan and Mace stood in the administrative office behind reception at the guesthouse. As they peered at the monitor on the desk, multiple views from the video cameras on the property appeared on the screen.

Tristan leaned in closer. "All of the cameras are up and running."

"Looks good from here," Mace said. "With the angle adjustments, you have a better view of the entrances and exits."

"Thanks for giving a hand with this." Not only had they made the adjustments, they'd also loaded new software that allowed Tristan to pull up the video feed from his desktop at the cottage and the stable, and Zurie to do the same from her office located down the hall from the restaurant and the upstairs suite she stayed in at the guesthouse.

"No problem. I have to work today and stopping here was on the way." Mace, already dressed in his uniform, glanced at a call buzzing in on his cell and hit Ignore. "One more thing you should add to your security plan is a nighttime guard working the grave-yard shift to monitor all of this and patrol the property."

"I agree. I'll speak to Zurie about adding it to the budget."

"Do you want me to talk to her?"

The offer was tempting. Zurie actually listened to Mace and easily took his advice. Funny considering she used to boss Mace around when he was younger.

"I won't have a problem getting her on board. When I talked to her last night, she was really concerned about what happened with E.J."

"Did you get a chance to see E.J. and his father before they left?"

"I did, but he wasn't in the mood to talk. It seemed like he just wanted to get home, but things seemed better between the two of them."

"Good. We were lucky he didn't wander too far off and that you and Chloe found him." Mace pointed to an image in the corner of the screen at a woman walking past the front desk outside the closed door of the office. "That's Chloe, isn't it?"

Tristan didn't need a closer look. His palms prac-tically itched as he recalled caressing her lush curves as he kissed her.

"So how's she doing?" Mace's inquisitive expres-sion made the question more than just a casual one.

"I guess she's fine. I haven't seen her until now."

"Oh?"

"Why do you look so surprised?"

"From the way you and she were acting yesterday, I thought maybe something was going on between the two of you."

Denying it would have been easy, but yesterday, if they would have finished what they'd started and not been interrupted, that would have been impossible to ignore. "Something did happen. I kissed her again."

"Again? Back up. When did you kiss her the first time?"

"At the restaurant, when we called a truce after the dart game."

Mace chuckled. "A truce. Is that what kissing a pretty woman is called now?"

"It wasn't like that. It was supposed to help us get past the distraction of wanting to kiss each other so we could focus on what was important." At the time, it made sense but hearing himself say that now, it didn't, plus the look on Mace's face confirmed it. "No need to comment on that. I already know what you're going to say."

Mace crossed his arms over his chest and leaned back against the edge of the desk. "Well, now that you know that theory is a total bust, what are the two of you going to do about it. Or are you just going to keep denying you like each other. It was obvious to me when the two of you walked to the guesthouse holding hands after you found the boy."

"Holding hands? No, we were—"

The moment Mace had recalled played through Tristan's mind. He'd reached out to make sure she made it over the puddle, after that…he hadn't thought twice about still holding on to her. It had felt so natural.

"Sure we like each other, but I've got a stable to run. She has an audition to get ready for. And she's going back to Hollywood in a few weeks. It doesn't make sense for us to get involved."

"Who are you trying to convince? You or me? 'Cause if it's me, you don't have to. You just admitted that the ignore-and-deny strategy isn't working. Why are you guys stressing yourselves out over nothing? Just go for it."

"And then what? After it's over, the next time I see her is on a movie screen or one night watching Netflix? It's too complicated. Letting a relationship get inside my head, I don't need that kind of problem right now."

Mace shrugged. "You honestly don't know if it will be a problem, but that's part of taking a risk."

"You're telling me to take a risk in a relationship? When it comes to your job, you'll take the risk all day, every day, but when it comes to women." A chuckle blew past Tristan's lips. "The only thing you'll risk is a one night hookup, maybe two nights if you really like her. Outside of that, you'll take zero risks."

Mace sobered. "If I could be with the woman I want to be with, I would."

The seriousness in his expression made Tristan pause. Mace had said *the* woman like he was speaking of someone specifically. He and Mace had been friends for almost fifteen years and stayed close even when he was in the army at the same time Mace was serving in the Marines. As far as he knew, like him,

Mace had around two long-term relationships that had lasted maybe a little over a year, but that was it and nothing recent. Who was she?

"So is this a real woman we're talking about that you'd take this risk with or a hypothetical one?"

Mace's faint smile indicated he wasn't taking the bait. "If you're leading up to asking me my advice, my answer is—if you really like Chloe, and you have an opportunity to spend time with her now—take the risk."

Chapter Seventeen

Tristan peered from under the brim of his black Stetson. A crowd of close to eighty enjoyed food and conversation at the tables set up under one of the two large tents near the pavilion just off the south pasture for Tillbridge's annual Spring Fling.

It wasn't mandatory for the staff to attend the noon to five Wednesday event but almost everyone had shown up. Some acknowledged the theme with just a cowboy hat while others went all out from the hat to a Western-style shirt to cowboy boots. A few spouses and significant others had also taken time off to join in and there were a few young children in the mix.

Philippa walked between the two buffet tables under the other nearby tent like a general inspecting her troops, making sure there was an endless supply of coleslaw, potato salad, corn bread and other side dishes along with the grilled chicken and her much anticipated smoked prime rib.

Other tables were laden with Rina's pies, cupcakes, and brownies and assorted beverages, and a far table had navy-and-white gift bags for each of the staff.

Rina walked up beside him wearing a beige cowboy hat. "We done good. Too bad Zurie isn't here to see it. This is our biggest one yet." She smiled softly. "I think they would have loved it."

By they, she meant their parents. When they'd first started holding the event, Jacob and Mathew had been the ones manning the grill, while Aunt Cherie had organized the side dishes with the help of the staff. Someone's friend, uncle or cousin, who considered themselves a DJ, had provided the music, and he, Rina and Zurie had been responsible for keeping the coolers filled with ice and soda, and the pitchers topped off with iced tea and lemonade.

Today Philippa was completely in charge of the food. Her cooks had helped prepare most of it the day before, but staff borrowed from a friend's catering company were actually cooking and working the event to give her people a break. There was still music—a local DJ was set up on the far end of the pavilion with space for people to dance, and they played horseshoes, cornhole and ball games with the kids.

One thing was missing. Mathew, Jacob and their fathers' friends sharing "back in the day" rodeo stories. Hearing about how they'd won buckles and awards, despite the hardships they'd faced, had given him the will to literally pick his butt up from the dirt.

Rina nudged him before she walked off. "Relax and grab a plate. Everyone's having a good time."

Everyone. Aside from stories of the past, there was also one person missing who he'd expected to see. Chloe.

He hadn't talked to her or really seen her since the weekend. He'd had meetings in Baltimore that had required him to stay overnight. After that, he'd been busy overseeing setup and other details for the Spring Fling.

Calling her had crossed his mind more than once, but what if she wasn't interested in "taking a risk" with him?

Just as he was about to ask Rina about her, Chloe walked into the area. She'd released her hair from the ponytail she'd been wearing lately and her dark wavy curls brushed her shoulders. A peach sundress highlighted her rich brown skin. The skirt of it fluttered above her knees. She wore cowboy boots. Once again, a vision of her wearing his Stetson appeared and his heart thumped a little harder in his chest.

Adam and Blake waved and called her over to their table where they sat with other grooms, trainers and staff from the restaurant.

Smiling, she joined them and took a seat. In less than a minute, one of them had handed her a beer and someone else had passed her a chocolate-frosted cupcake. She was immediately enveloped into their conversation.

But what if she viewed that last kiss under the run-in, and what almost happened, as a result from finding E.J.? That it had just been an impulse that they'd acted upon to release the tension and adrenaline after they'd found him?

He'd actually considered that as the reason. But hell, Tillbridge was on his mind and schedule 24/7. He hadn't gotten involved with a woman, seriously, over the past two years because he couldn't give her the time and attention she deserved. If she did want to be with him, what did he have to offer her over the next few weeks she was at Tillbridge?

The friendly, animated banter at the table grew louder. Chloe laughed along with everyone as she licked frosting from her fingers.

What she was enjoying with her friends, having a good time, she wouldn't want to give that up for the few hours here and there he'd be able to give her. Would she? A strange empty sensation of doubt that he'd never felt before opened in his gut. It was tempting to have another beer and try to drink the feeling away. He couldn't.

What Mace had said that past Sunday had really made him think. Could he accept her leaving without even taking a shot at being with her for the time they had left?

Chloe finished the cupcake and was hit with the giddy warmth of a sugar rush. Or was the rush from seeing Tristan when she'd first walked in?

Now she understood why her hair stylist at home swore by three Instagram accounts to get her past a lonely weekend: hot men holding tiny creatures like babies, kittens and puppies, hot men in uniform and hot cowboys.

Chloe could vouch for the latter. How could any woman not notice him? He was all kinds of sexy from his hat to the light gray button-down tucked into his jeans to his dark boots.

Only seeing brief glimpses of him at the stable for the past couple of days had been nothing short of frustrating. Especially since she couldn't stop wondering how he'd felt about their kiss over the weekend. And those photos of him in full cowboy gear that Rina had showed her that past Sunday hadn't helped the cause of staying focused on horses instead of him.

Maybe she should pull him aside later and ask if they could talk about it. But what would she say to him? That she was glad things hadn't gone further? That a moment like that couldn't happen again?

Her gaze wandered to where she'd spotted him when she first walked in standing near the pavilion with Rina. As always, he was on the move, stopping to talk to Philippa before heading off to undoubtedly handle some needed task. As busy as he was, maybe they didn't have to worry about anything happening again. His schedule would solve the problem by ensuring they weren't in proximity of each other. Her heart sank in her chest with a deep thump.

"You eating?" Adam sat next to Chloe at the eight-seat folding table. He was preparing to head to the buffet. "If you want prime rib, you should hurry. It'll be gone soon."

Blake sitting across from them snorted a laugh. "Yeah, Chloe, you better hurry. Considering how many times he's been to the buffet, I'm surprised there's anything left."

"Whatever, dude." Adam balled up a paper napkin and tossed it at Blake. "Your plate hasn't exactly been empty either."

More teasing went back and forth, but in the end, she and Adam ended up agreeing to bring back chicken, prime rib and corn bread for the table.

While they were at the buffet, the DJ switched from an upbeat instrumental mix to popular dance music with lyrics familiar to the crowd. The mood amped up a little as people got up to dance.

Chloe couldn't help but move just a little to the beat while she held empty plates that Adam loaded with the requested food items.

He glanced over. "Someone's up for dancing."

"Yeah, I might get out there."

"Might? I'll drag you out there if I have to."

Adam was so darn sweet. She'd been careful not to encourage what she sensed was a possible crush on her. "Won't Bethany mind?"

Last she'd heard, the two had started going out with each other. She watched for any signs that Bethany minded her being friends with Adam. Chloe hadn't picked up on any bad vibes from Bethany, so far, but for some girlfriends, their man dancing with another woman was strictly off-limits, and Chloe wasn't about to violate girl code.

He glanced at the table they'd just left. Bethany sat

next to his empty seat. He grinned. "No. She won't. Bethany will probably be out there before both of us."

While they were still eating at the table, Bethany jumped up to dance with a blond trainer that worked at the stable, one of the male servers and a front desk clerk.

Chloe had barely finished her food when Bethany was motioning to Adam that the two of them should join them on the dance floor.

"Go ahead." Chloe waved him on.

A group dance song from way back blasted through the speakers.

A collective cheer rose from the group. Staff members of Tillbridge jumped up from the tables around them and headed for the floor.

"You have to dance to this one." Adam grinned as he pulled her along with him. "It's tradition."

He wasn't lying.

Blake, Rina, Philippa, even Gloria jumped up, leaving her husband at a nearby table, to take a place in line, following the lyrics to roll it, cha-cha and two-step turn.

As Chloe stepped right like the song said, she spotted Tristan returning from whatever errand he'd left to do.

Everyone else saw him, too, shouting for him to come to the dance floor.

Would he?

He didn't seem like the dancing type, but with a slight smile on his face, he walked to the line ahead of her, and without missing a step, he joined in.

Tristan moved his hips with a casual ease.

Chloe's mouth went dry as she stared.

He hit the next cue for a two-step turn, but she missed hers.

Bethany grabbed her by the shoulders and pointed her in the right direction. Her nape tingled as she thought of Tristan, now behind her.

The song transitioned into a more recent group dance song. The floor cleared out a little as Rina and Philippa and a few others sat down, but Chloe remained and so did Tristan.

The now shorter lines compressed and Tristan ended up right in front of her.

Breathe, baby girl, just breathe. He wasn't the first man she'd witnessed on the dance floor with all the right assets, but she could barely remember the steps the lyrics called for with him so close.

Chloe glanced over and caught him looking at her. Before she could stop herself, the sassy girl inside of her took over, and she put a little more movement in her hips. Was it her imagination or had he put a little more swagger in his?

A breeze blew over her, wicking away a small bit of moisture on her hairline. Usually, that was her cue to stop dancing and cool off, but she didn't want to. Every left and right step, dip, sway and turn seemed to bring their steps in perfect sync. Even when the song switched to a new line dance she didn't know well to a song with a pop-country flair, she hung in, not caring if she didn't execute it perfectly. It felt almost as if she was just dancing with him instead of with everyone else on the floor.

"All right, people," the DJ called out over the mic. "I've gotten a few requests to change it up."

A country song pumped through the speakers, and Adam, Bethany and other couples paired up.

Well, the fun was over. Chloe reluctantly started to head back to her seat and almost ran into Tristan. A small shudder of awareness zipped through her.

She stared up at him, suddenly unable to speak, searching his face for a sign or an inkling that she wasn't the only one who'd felt it. Chloe didn't realize her hand was raised in his or that his other hand rested on her back until a dancing couple bumped her closer to him.

Chloe held on to his arm for balance. He wanted to dance with her. "But I don't know this one."

Tristan leaned in near her ear. "I'll teach you. Trust me. It's not complicated."

Not complicated? Every cell of her being was awakened by his proximity and his familiar scent warming on his skin. She'd probably make a fool of herself. "Okay. I'll try."

He moved back a little. "It's just a simple two-step. When I step forward with my left foot, you step back with your right. Then it's quick-quick, slow-slow. Quick-quick, slow-slow. I'll guide you through it."

Right away, she jumbled the steps.

Tristan chuckled. "Wait. Let's do that again. Start with your other right."

Meaning not her left foot. Instead of cringing with

embarrassment the humor in his expression made her laugh, and she tried again. A few steps later, she followed his lead finally easing into the smooth easy movements without stepping on the toes of his boots.

He caught her off guard as he released her and twirled her around. When he took her back into his arms, her leg slid between his, aligning their hips and melding her to his chest...just like during their kiss in the pasture.

Nearby, Adam and Bethany danced just as close. When Adam spun her around, in one deft move, Bethany snagged his brown cowboy hat from his head and put it on hers. Bethany wound her arms around Adam's neck, and he rested his forehead to hers as his hands slid to her waist.

A hint of envy filled Chloe as she longed for that kind of intimacy with Tristan, but unlike Bethany and Adam, that kind of closeness would put all eyes on them, making people wonder about them, and raise questions that she didn't even have the answer to about her relationship status with Tristan.

Needing to change focus, Chloe looked to his cowboy hat. His other hat was in the front seat of her rental, parked just off the road near the pasture gate along with the cars of other Spring Fling attendees. She'd planned to hand it over to him after the party.

"Your Stetson reminds me, I need to give you your ball cap back."

"Or you could trade up."

"What exactly does 'trade up' mean?" The huskiness in his voice made her look directly into his eyes.

Tristan's slow lean in near her cheek brought her closer to him, and she drew in an unsteady breath as his lightly whiskered cheek grazed hers. "You tell me."

At the end of the party, Chloe pitched in with everyone else cleaning up the pavilion.

She hadn't talked or been near Tristan after they'd danced together, but like a sixth sense that she'd just developed during the party, she knew exactly where he was, helping the DJ load his equipment into the back of a trailer hooked to a van.

Her gaze kept drifting to meet his. It had been that way for hours, even in the midst of them holding conversations with other people.

You tell me.

She'd asked the question, and he'd given her an answer. Now it was her turn to respond.

A short time later, the staff and their families said their goodbyes. One by one, cars pulled onto the road illuminated by the late-evening sun as everyone headed home.

"You sure I can't talk you into taking these?" Rina pointed to the paper plate filled with brownies in her hand as the two of them walked out the pasture gate, headed for their cars.

"Thanks, but no. They're too good. I'll just eat every single one of them." Or not. The fluttery feeling tumbling inside of her as she'd thought of Tristan didn't leave room for anything else.

"Why do you think I don't want to ride back with them." Rina laughed as she got into her bluish-gray four-door sedan. "I think I'll drop them off at the sheriff's office on the way home. See you later."

Chloe opened the door to her car that was parked two empty spaces over from Tristan's.

His hat sat on the front passenger seat. She reached over and picked it up, and when she stood straight, she glanced over her shoulder.

Tristan walked toward her.

Her heart sped up as the last of the cars drove away. They were alone.

As he stood in front of Chloe, he gave her one of his small, sexy smiles. "Is that for me, Ace?"

His gaze dropped to the ball cap clutched in her hand.

She could give him the hat and endure weeks of pretending the kisses they'd shared didn't matter, but the truth was, she wished for more. But unlike the brownies, she couldn't just not indulge. She was tired of trying. And as far as answering his question, sometimes it was better to let actions speak louder than words.

Chloe took his Stetson off his head and put it on hers. As he stared into her eyes, she raised up on her toes and kissed him.

Chapter Eighteen

Anticipation made Chloe tremble as Tristan shut the back door of his cottage behind them. They leaned on opposite walls in the entryway.

Four solid thunks echoed in the small space as their boots, along with their socks, hit the floor.

Finally, they could give in to the invisible but tangible connection that had been teasing and taunting them for weeks.

He reached for her and she went to him, immediately winding her arms around his neck. He swooped under the brim of his cowboy hat, still resting on her head, and covered her mouth firmly with his.

Desire flowed through her with a deepening kiss. In between teasing nips and brushes over each other's lips, they shuffled down the back hallway into the kitchen.

A few steps past the stove, he picked her straight up, and a small squeal shot out of her. The hat fell off as he carried her the rest of the way down the side hall leading to the bedroom. As she grasped onto his shoulders and looked down at him, the sexual hunger in his eyes made her heart beat harder. He was just as impatient for this as she was.

As soon as they made it past the threshold, he partially released her and she slid down his torso. The slow drag of her fabric covered nipples down his hard pecs awakened nerve endings. Her breasts felt full and heavy. Her feet touched the floor and as he kissed her, longing slowly and sweetly grew inside of her.

Tristan glided his hands down her back to cup her butt and bring her firmly against him. The feel of his jean-covered erection against her lower abdomen stole a breath.

He trailed kisses from her cheek down the side of her neck. "I need you."

The heat from his openmouthed kisses made her shiver. "I need you, too."

They both reached for the top button of his shirt at the same time. In between more feverish kisses, she unbuttoned from the bottom up while he tore at the buttons from the top down. Finally they were done and he shrugged the shirt off.

She sucked in a breath, struck motionless, admiring what she'd only been able to dream of for too many long days and nights. Perfection. Chloe pressed her lips to his chest and soaked in the heat of him with her lips and fingertips, caressing over the dips and valleys of his abs. Her hand came to the button on his jeans and she popped it open.

He interrupted her plans by pulling up the hem of her dress. She raised her arms, making it easier for him to lift it up and over her head.

As he dropped her dress to the floor, his jawline angled with his heated gaze. His eyes stayed on her as she popped open the front closure of her beige lace bra and took it off along with her matching bikinis. As if he was transfixed, he took her in from her head to her polished pink toenails.

Tristan reached out and glided his palms over the outer swells of her breasts, down her rib cage, and through the dips of her waist.

Her legs grew weak and as she swayed forward, he pulled her to him. "You're so beautiful." The huskiness of his voice flowed over her smooth, warm, and wonderful like his caresses.

"You are, too." Chloe glided her arms up his chest and around his neck.

She grasped his nape and kissed him. The new sensation of being with him skin to skin made desire, heady and hot, uncoil.

Tristan turned her around and urged her backward. The backs of her knees hit the mattress, and he followed her down on the bed. Every brush of his lips—from the notch in the middle of her throat to the swells and peaks of her breasts, down her belly, and moving lower—made her ache.

Chloe arched up underneath him, losing herself in erotic sensation. Was it possible to die from so much pleasure? By the time he stripped off his boxer briefs and jeans, and sheathed himself in a condom, she was lost in it and craving more.

Tristan thrust inside of her, setting a slow pace that pulled out her moans, gasps…made her beg. He kissed down her cheek to nip her earlobe and whispered, "Not yet."

She followed his lead and wrapped her legs around his hips. Her heart pounded as she matched his quickening rhythm, holding on to him as his back muscles bunched underneath her palms.

Pleasure began to unfurl from her toes, rising inside of her, making her cry out his name as she climaxed. Soon after, he found his release.

"Thanks for letting me borrow your shirt." Chloe snuggled next to Tristan in his bed with her head on his bare shoulder.

"You're welcome." He wrapped an arm around her, holding her close.

Just like with his hats, she looked good in his black T-shirt, too, and the fact that she'd accepted it from him when she'd gotten out of the shower, versus putting on her dress, meant she wasn't in a hurry to leave.

Maybe it was because of the weather. He glanced to the side window. The sun had set a couple of hours ago and the corner floor lamp illuminated the rain, trailing down the glass. It fell steadily, drumming a quiet beat on the roof of the cottage.

Or maybe it felt just as right to her to be there as it

did to him to hold her in his arms, no longer denying the attraction that existed between them.

Chloe traced a lazy pattern in the middle of his chest, raising tingles and need.

He glanced down at her, but she wasn't paying attention to him or what she was causing to happen below his waist. Her focus was on the photos sitting on the dresser against the wall. She'd glanced over them earlier when he was looking for a T-shirt to give her.

Tristan kissed her forehead. "What's that frown about?"

"Am I frowning?" She laughed. "I didn't realize it. Nothing really. I was just wondering."

"About?"

"Your cowboy hat. Is it the same one in the photos?"

"It's one of them. A few got crushed by a bull who got the best of me."

She slightly shuddered. "Better your hat than you. Rina mentioned you were the only one in your family who chose bull riding as a sport. Why? Who turned you on to doing it?"

He didn't pick up any judgment in her tone. Just curiosity. Still he tipped up her chin to look into her eyes and steal a quick kiss. "For years my father didn't just work at the stable. He was also an off-site sales rep for a company that sold tractors and other heavy equipment to farms and ranches. Growing up, sometimes, I'd go with him to visit clients during my summer school break."

As much as he loved the family atmosphere at the house, he looked forward to those rare overnight trips in the car with just him and his dad. His father could stick to one topic for hours—the pros and cons of the types of cars on the interstate, what it took to build a house, the ups and down of politics, competitions he'd been in, how to close a business deal—and he'd never grown tired listening to him.

Tristan continued, focusing on answering Chloe's question. "One day we were in Kentucky, and we stopped at a place where the owner was a former bull rider. He was coaching his son and another guy from Brazil to ride. It wasn't that I hadn't seen it done before, but for some reason, that day, it clicked. I told my dad I wanted to learn."

"So that's when you started calf riding, right?"

"Yeah, let me guess. When you went to Rina's she pulled out at least five albums and bored you with pictures?"

"Not five of them, just two." Chloe grinned. "And it wasn't boring. I liked looking at all of those cute pictures of a younger you."

"Don't tell her that or she'll lure you back to her place to go through her entire album and memorabilia collection. Five albums is a conservative estimate, and that's not including scrapbooks and the pictures filed away on her laptop and phone. The only upside is the cocktails she'll make for you."

"Oh, stop." Chloe playfully poked him in the side. "I think it's great that Rina has the history of your family in one place." She rose from his chest and propped herself up on her elbow beside him. "Why did you stop bull riding?"

"The first time?" He rested an arm behind his head. "I joined the military. There wasn't a whole lot of opportunities for it."

"And after that?"

Yeah, he'd opened the door to that by saying "the first time." Usually, he was more concise with his response to that question, but with Chloe, it had just come out.

But no matter how easy it was to talk to her, now wasn't the time for the long answer to that question. It contained drama, chaos and gut-twisting turns that would ruin the moment.

He faced her, propping his elbow underneath him. "The second time was for the stable. I needed to take my place here." She went to ask another question, but he briefly laid a finger to her lips. "Enough about me, tell me about you. Did you always want to be an actress?"

From the look in her eyes, he hadn't fooled her. She realized he was purposely diverting the conversation. "I don't know about always, although I did play Moses in a church play when I was six. I ran around practicing parting the Red Sea for weeks wearing a gray beard." She lowered her tone. "Speaking in a deep ominous voice." Chloe laughed. "I drove my older brother, Thad, and my parents nuts."

A vision of a pint-sized Chloe wearing the beard raised a chuckle in Tristan. "What finally made you stop doing it?"

"The neighbor's dog ate Moses's beard." Her eyes

narrowed playfully. "But I'm pretty sure my big brother had something to do with it."

"It's great that your family is so supportive of your career."

Her smile faded. "More like tolerant. They're not exactly thrilled that I didn't join the family business." The teasing tone she was trying for wasn't quite there.

"What type of company is it?"

"Not a company, a profession. My dad's a cardiologist. My mom is a dietitian. And Thad, he's a paramedic." She plucked at a loose thread on the pillow case. "They're a little more supportive of me now than when I started. But from their point of view, the careers they've chosen are sensible and serve a practical purpose. Mine doesn't. I think on some level they expect me to show up on their doorstep with my stuff in moving boxes, ready to admit I made a mistake and that I need their help to start over."

She was so driven as an actress, he'd assumed her parents had instilled that in her by rallying around her like his family had done for him when he was younger. But during competitions, he'd also witnessed inner drive coming from too much judgment. Some succeeded. Others couldn't get out of their heads long enough to move forward because they were always hyperanalyzing their performances. The rest usually pushed too hard and wound up with injuries, in some cases those injuries had been career ending.

It was hard to imagine what Chloe was telling him, but the slightly sad expression on her face confirmed it.

He glided his finger down her cheek. "When they're

watching you give your acceptance speech for the award you're going to win for this movie you're auditioning for, I bet that will change their minds."

Her smile came back with a laugh. "Yeah, that could do it." She cleared her throat and mocked holding an award and looking sincerely into a camera. "I'm so honored to accept this. And I must give a huge thank-you to Moonlight Joy and Thunder Bay for making it possible. I couldn't have done it without them."

"Wait a minute." He took advantage of her being slightly off-balance and rolled Chloe under him. "Thunder gets a thank-you but I don't?"

She laughed. "I'm starting to like him a little better."

"And his owner?" He kissed her and need grew inside of him as she glided her silky-smooth legs over his.

Chloe smiled against his lips. "I like him even more."

Chapter Nineteen

Late Saturday afternoon, Tristan sat at his desk in the office at the stable.

Gloria, deep into some report, tapped away on her computer.

They usually worked a few hours on Saturday, but this time they had a little more catching up to do after taking off for the Spring Fling party.

He was supposed to be reviewing the care journals for the horses, but as hard as he tried, he couldn't stop his mind from wandering to Chloe. He hadn't really seen her since Wednesday. The next workday had been busy, and she'd already had dinner plans with staff from the guesthouse.

Unable to sleep, he'd given in to calling her later that night to see how her day had been.

They'd talked about a few things, including childhood pranks. Apparently one of the waitstaff she'd gone to dinner with was exasperated with her young son. He'd scared her awake that morning by leaving a huge plastic spider for her to find in the shower.

Did you pull any pranks when you were a kid or were you a Goody Two-shoes? Chloe had asked over the phone.

No, I definitely wasn't a Goody Two-shoes. One weekend, our parents were away, and I'd been put in charge of making breakfast for me, Zurie and Rina...

Telling the story of how he'd frozen the cereal and milk in bowls overnight, and in the morning, poured a little milk on the top so they wouldn't notice when they sat down at the table to eat their Sugar Pops, had almost made him laugh just as hard as it had then. Especially as he remembered Zurie's and Rina's bewildered expressions when they'd first tried to dig into the frozen bowls with their spoons.

He hadn't thought about that day in a long time. It had felt good to share it and recall the fun they'd had growing up together.

He and Chloe had then moved on to random topics that popped up.

Her favorite color—she couldn't settle on just one: pink, peach or red, depending on her mood. His: navy blue. His favorite holiday—Thanksgiving. Hers was Halloween. She loved dressing up and going to parties. Recent trips: Him to Kentucky to deliver a horse that had been boarded at the stable to its owner's new home. Her to New York to see the musical *Hamilton*.

Yesterday had been another busy day, and that evening, he'd had to attend a business mixer the mayor of Bolan had hosted. When he'd gotten back home, Chloe had called him, and once again they'd talked for hours. He'd awakened tired in the morning but also happy they'd made dinner plans.

In some ways, it felt as if they'd wasted time not being together, and now they were playing catch-up, trying to fit in all they'd missed. But it was impossible to fit it all in the time they had left before she was heading back to California. That was something he was trying not to think about too hard, and instead, just do what Mace had suggested. Enjoy as much of now with Chloe as he could. Which was a good reason to finish work so he could get to her.

He refocused on Jumping Jett's report on his wide computer screen. Wes had recently stopped by and he was pleased with Jett's progress.

Tristan's phone buzzed with a text. It was Chloe.

Still on for dinner at six?

He tapped in a response.

Yes. See u soon.

Ninety more minutes. How long until he'd see Chloe again just naturally calculated in his mind. He couldn't stop doing it, along with the grin that also took over his face at the same time.

"You haven't heard a word I said," Gloria interjected, pulling him out of his thoughts.

"Sorry, I got caught up reading Jett's progress report. Everything looks really good. We're on the right supplement track with him."

"Uh-huh." She gave him her patented stare over her glasses, but there was also an amused knowing look in her eyes. "Considering how long you've been staring at it, you should have the report memorized. You might as well leave now and enjoy your plans for the weekend."

Plans. She meant Chloe, didn't she? But he hadn't talked about the change in their relationship with anyone, not even Mace. He and Chloe hadn't discussed it, but they hadn't put their new status on blast either.

Although he never shared about his private life with the staff, Gloria was more like family. "So you know about me and Chloe?"

"Of course I do. You switching from being Thunder's evil twin around her to staring into space with a sappy grin on your face wasn't exactly a small clue. It's about time you stopped being a hermit."

"I'm not a hermit. I've taken a few women out this year."

"Notice I said a hermit not a monk." She focused back on her computer screen, tapping on the keyboard. "You've had your diversions, but Chloe is different. She's right here at Tillbridge. You'll be seeing a lot of each other. At least until she leaves. When does she have to go back to California?"

"In about three weeks." Saying it aloud shaved off a layer of happiness.

"That's not a lot of time. Sounds a lot like an eight-second bull ride to me. You know how it goes. Staying focused on what's important. Maximizing your time before it ends."

He could read between the lines of what she wasn't saying. It sounded like she and Mace were using the same relationship handbook. But if she was telling him he should leave to be with Chloe, he'd gladly take Gloria's advice. Tristan closed the file he'd been scanning. He'd finish reading through the reports on Monday.

"I'm heading out." He stood. "Don't work too long. Go home and enjoy your grandbabies." Gloria and her husband loved to spoil the toddler-aged girl and boy and usually spent weekends with their daughter and son-in-law who lived near them.

As he headed out the door, Gloria called, "Tristan."

"Yes, ma'am." His response was lighthearted but it also came with a dose of respect.

She looked up at him. "Don't forget, when it comes to you and Chloe, the clock doesn't have to stop. Unless you want it to."

Chapter Twenty

Chloe glanced over at Tristan as he pulled into the full parking lot of the Montecito Steakhouse.

It was another busy night. A crowd mingled on the front porch area of the dark wood and brick restaurant where she and Tristan had shared their first kiss.

He'd been quiet the entire drive there. When she'd asked him if something had happened at the stable or guesthouse, he'd said everything was fine. But he was clearly distracted. Did it have something to do with the two of them not staying in for another night at his place as they'd originally planned? She'd been the one to suggest going out to dinner. When she'd picked the Montecito, she'd forgotten it was a popular local spot. Maybe he wasn't comfortable with them going there.

During their few days together, they hadn't ventured into the "what are we" conversation or if they were making whatever it was public or not.

Tristan backed in a corner space. As he shut off the engine of his SUV, he glanced over at her and smiled. "Ready?"

"Sure." She was probably making something out of nothing. It was just dinner, not a big deal.

As they walked toward the entrance, the casual clothes everyone had on caught her attention.

Suddenly the burgundy halter dress that would have fit in as casual in LA felt too fashionable, too short and too warm all at once. But he looked a little more dressed up than usual, too, in his dark jeans and black Henley.

The stiletto heel of her strappy burgundy sandal raked over a crack in the pavement, and she took a slightly uneven step.

Tristan rested his hand on her lower back and curled his fingers into her waist. His gaze dropped to her feet, then rose to her eyes. "You look great."

The male appreciation she saw in his gaze erased any doubts about whether or not she'd chosen the right dress.

But as soon as they walked into the corridor between the bar and the dining area of the Montecito, the more than a few curious stares made her self-conscious again.

From the way they were dressed, they should have also worn signs proclaiming "we're on a date." But they weren't really dating, just temporarily spending time together.

Chloe was used to people gawking at her, usually because she looked familiar, but she wasn't famous enough for them to realize they'd watched her on television or saw her for a brief moment in a movie. But tracking her and Tristan's progress, as they walked through the tables and past booths in the space with chocolate-brown walls trimmed with beige brick, seemed to be more interesting to people than the food on the menu.

She felt like a goldfish in a bowl as they slid into the padded pleather booth halfway down the sidewall.

Tristan made a quick glance around the room and nodded at a few people. From the way his brows slightly pulled together, as he scanned the menu, he'd noticed the overabundance of glances coming their way, too. "What's catching your attention?"

Aside from Wes and an older woman leaning out of the booth farther down to stare at them? "The petite filet and shrimp looks good."

"I think I'll have the rib eye."

Ten minutes after they ordered, Wes came over to their booth with the thin woman who he introduced as his wife, Nora.

From the strength of her handshake, Nora definitely wasn't as fragile as she looked. Gentle creases formed in the golden-brown-skinned woman's face with her pleasant smile. "You two look nice. Special occasion?" Her raised brow practically spelled "fishing expedition."

Tristan glanced at Chloe before he answered. "We're just enjoying a night out."

"Oh, that's nice." She kept smiling at them as if she expected them to say more.

"Well, we just wanted to say hello." Wes reached for Nora's arm, and the way she jabbed him in the stomach with her bony elbow made Chloe wince.

Nora leaned in as she looked to Chloe. "So I hear you're visiting from Los Angeles. Bolan must be a big change for you."

"It's nice. I like it here."

"Nice enough to come back for another visit?" Her gaze slid over to Tristan for a moment.

"Uh...maybe?" Chloe hadn't really thought about it.

"Okay, Nora. Time to stop playing twenty questions and let them enjoy themselves." Wes nodded and smiled at them as he grasped Nora firmly by the shoulders and moved her along.

After Wes left, more people associated with the stable, as well as local people she didn't know, but who were acquainted with Tristan, stopped by their table. Although none of them were bold enough to outright ask if they were seeing each other, just like with Wes and his wife, their curiosity was obvious. Not to mention the hushed conversations the people had as they walked away.

Their food finally arrived, but with all of the interruptions between bites, it grew cold. Chloe slid her half-full plate away and so did Tristan. They skipped dessert.

As he asked for the check, Tristan didn't look pleased, but it couldn't have been about the service or the food, both had been great.

Chloe made a trip to the ladies' room. As she reached the end of the hall leading back out to the restaurant, she ran into Mace, most likely headed for the men's room.

He smiled as he greeted her, but he gave off an official and capable vibe in his uniform. "You plan on kicking Tristan's tail again in a dart game tonight?"

"No, we just came for dinner, nothing special." She scooted to the side so a woman could pass them. "What are you doing here?"

"Meal break." Mace glanced at another officer in a booth down from the one where Tristan waited for her. "How's the food? Sometimes when we stop by here, and it's this busy, the quality is a little iffy."

"The steak and shrimp I had was good."

"I'll give it a try. I'm surprised Tristan didn't take you to Baltimore. The restaurants at the harbor are really good."

"This was a last-minute thing." She almost added that it wasn't a date.

"I see." He studied her for a beat and his smile widened. "I'm glad you got him away from Tillbridge. You're the first person to get him to relax and enjoy himself in a long time." Mace touched her arm, an innocent friendly gesture. "I'll let you get back to him."

Mace had mentioned Tristan relaxing and enjoying himself, but he'd been mistaken. Tristan seemed anything but relaxed as he ushered her out of the restaurant.

Once they were in the car, Tristan released a breath as if he'd been holding it.

Her choice of going out had ruined their night.

"I'm sorry." They both blurted it out at the same time.

Her surprise mirrored what she saw on his face. "Why are you apologizing?"

He reached over and took her hand. "You didn't get a chance to enjoy dinner because everyone kept bothering us. I knew people might be curious, but I didn't expect them to stare like that and keep coming to our table."

"But I was the one who suggested coming here. It was my fault for picking a place that would put you on the spot about us being together."

"On the spot? You think I didn't want people to know about us?"

Uncertainty made her shrug. "I guess. I don't know. I mean no PDA around the stable or guesthouse seemed like a no-brainer. As far as telling people anything…"

"I agree that we shouldn't be all over each other while we're working, beyond that, I say we do whatever we want. I'm happy that we're together."

"You are? Really?"

"Really." He grinned.

Giddiness sparked in her chest. But she was being silly. It wasn't like he'd asked her to be his girlfriend.

"But we only have a few more weeks, and I want us to make the best of the time we have left together." He stared out the windshield at the Montecito. "Not having to contend with people bothering us."

"But it wasn't all bad." As she thought about dinner, something stood out. "I could tell that a lot of those people care about you. Like Wes and his wife. When they left, she was beaming at us like a proud parent. And everyone else just seemed happy to see you. Even Mace mentioned how it was good to see you taking time to enjoy yourself. You're lucky to have people who care about you like that."

"I guess you're right."

She was right. The one thing she enjoyed about Tillbridge was that the staff was tight-knit like a close family. Sure, there were a few employees who were mainly out for themselves, but overall, the caring spirit they shared was genuine. She'd miss that back in LA.

"Still, I'd like to go out with you and have a little privacy." Tristan intertwined their fingers. As he stared down at them a long moment, the same pensive expression that had been on his face during the drive to the restaurant returned. "I was wondering. What do you think about us going away somewhere? Maybe next weekend. We can relax and have time together without the interruptions."

A weekend away from Tillbridge. A chance to have some uninterrupted quality time with him. That sounded nice. "Are you sure you can take the time off?"

"I can make it work. What about you?"

She did have one minor task she couldn't ignore. "I just have a massive amount of laundry to get done sometime during the week. I'm almost out of clean clothes. Rina said I could do it at her place."

"Or you could do it at mine..." Tristan leaned across the console between the seats. "Starting tonight."

He pressed his lips to hers.

When they broke apart. She rested her forehead on his and closed her eyes, waiting for her heart to slow. "If I go home with you now, the only thing I'll be doing with clothes is not wearing them."

Tristan tipped up her chin. "I definitely don't see a problem with that."

One long, slow, mesmerizing kiss later…neither did she.

Chapter Twenty-One

The Saturday of her and Tristan's big weekend, Chloe pressed in the code Tristan had given her to open the back door of his cottage, juggling her purse, a purple overnight bag…and a net bag with her dirty clothes.

She had just enough time to do laundry before he came home from the stable. He had to put in a few hours of work before they could leave.

During the past week, her laundry plans had fallen through. One, from pure laziness. Two, she'd gotten the opportunity to travel around with Wes and the local large animal vet as they tended to not only horses but other livestock in the area. And three, anytime she'd had left, usually at night, she'd spent with Tristan where the priority for clothes really had been about not wearing them as soon as she arrived.

As she walked inside, and unburdened herself of the net bag in the laundry room on the right, she smiled as she reminisced about their nights together. Not the entire night, though. He woke up at four every morning. If she'd stayed, she would have been awake right along with him, wishing for more sleep. Being able to sleep in a little longer, in the same bed, was one of the things that would make this weekend even more wonderful.

Chloe carried her purse and mostly empty purple bag to the bedroom. She laid her things next to his medium-sized black duffel bag sitting on the gray comforter just below the slate-colored pillows covering the neatly made bed. It was unzipped but packed. A clear bag on top held his razor and shaving soap.

He still wouldn't give her any clues about where they were going. He'd said pack for a casual weekend, but in her experience, a guy's version of casual was usually different from hers. She was not only bringing a pair of cute tennis shoes and her cowboy boots but also a pair of pink stilettos and a cream linen shirt she could throw on with a pair of jeans if she needed an outfit with a little more "oomph."

They couldn't go too far away if they had only the weekend. Baltimore, maybe? Too bad they didn't have time for a longer getaway to someplace sunny and secluded with all the right amenities. If only they had more than a few days.

The sadness that came over her lately when she thought about leaving returned. She sat on the bed, absorbing the memories of his black Stetson and photos on the dresser. The soft light coming through the side window. The feel of the comforter as she glided her palm over it, and the clean scent of his soap.

A part of her hated that she had to return to California. But what had Tristan said to her last night? That he wanted them to enjoy the time they had left. She was projecting ahead and missing out on the best part of now. Now was about spending a wonderful, carefree weekend with Tristan.

Tristan pulled his 4Runner into the driveway at the back of the cottage and parked behind Chloe's rental.

She was already there, which meant they could leave right away…if she was done with her laundry. She'd claimed to have a massive amount of it. Too bad she couldn't do it where they were going instead. He couldn't wait to take her there. Happiness and an impatient need to hit the road grew inside of him.

He hadn't told her where they were going because up until that morning, he wasn't sure, so he'd picked two places. If she didn't like the first, he had a backup, but he really hoped she liked his first choice.

Just as he went to get out of the SUV, his phone rang. It was Gloria. He'd left her in charge along with Blake and Philippa. As he'd walked out of his office a short time ago, she'd said they wouldn't contact him unless something was really wrong.

Dread sank inside of him as he answered. "Hi, Gloria."

"Zurie just called. She told me to hunt you down because she hasn't been able to reach you."

When Zurie had phoned earlier, he'd been at the

arena with Blake, who was working with Jett, going over the schedule for the rest of the weekend and Monday morning. He and Chloe weren't planning to return until the afternoon.

"Did she say what she wanted?"

"Other than to talk to you, no. I told her to try calling you in five minutes."

His phone buzzed in with a call. It was Zurie.

"She's calling me now." Tristan released a long breath and shut his eyes. Maybe he could let the call go to voice mail, then send her a text telling her that he was busy, and that he'd call her late tomorrow or early Monday.

"If you want any peace, don't skip the phone call," Gloria interjected, as if she'd read his mind. How did she always do that? "Talk to her before you leave. And Tristan."

"Yes?"

"Lead with patience." She hung up.

Tristan answered the other line. "Hey, Zurie."

"Why are you dodging my calls? I've been trying to get in touch with you since yesterday."

"We have been in touch. You sent me a text yesterday asking questions about the budget for next quarter, which I answered. This morning, I was handling business in the stable."

"That's yesterday and today, what about the rest of the week? How am I supposed to stay up-to-date about what's going on there, if you're not making time to stay in contact with me?"

"Key word is time, Zurie. I'm doing my job and yours so that hasn't exactly left me with a lot of it."

"I didn't call to argue with you."

Could have fooled him. "Why did you call?"

Basic first-aid training for the staff, general maintenance on the air-conditioning units in preparation for the summer, cottage repairs—things that were on his radar or already handled but Zurie didn't bother to ask him what he'd already done. Instead she went over them, telling him what he should do or needed to do as if he didn't have a clue about how to handle them.

Patience. Gloria hadn't been kidding when she'd told him that earlier. He just listened. When she stopped talking, he said. "Got it. Anything else?"

"Yes. I have a lead on a gelding for the stable. The owner is in Augusta. He isn't actively trying to sell, but he's willing to let us buy the horse if we're interested."

"We should hold off on that. A guy I used to bull ride with has a horse he needs to sell in North Carolina. We were supposed to meet up in Baltimore to talk more about it, but then the boy got lost after the party that weekend. I had to cancel. He's on the road now, but I promised him we'd link up and discuss it."

"So you're keeping in touch with your old crowd? I didn't realize that." She didn't sound happy.

After all he'd just said, him keeping in touch with the people he used to bull ride with, that was the part she was concerned about? "I reach out every now and then, but he actually messaged me on Facebook."

"Fine. Talk to your friend, but I'd like to clear the horse in Augusta off my to-do list now."

"Consider it off your list and on mine. I'll handle it."

"We just need an hour. Gloria's a miracle worker. Tell her to shuffle some things around on your schedule."

He'd promised Chloe forty-eight hours of privacy, just the two of them, no unnecessary interruptions. There was no reason the call couldn't wait. "Today or tomorrow won't work for me. I won't be back on the property until Monday afternoon. I'm taking time off."

"You're taking a vacation now? While I'm gone?" She said it as if he was committing a crime.

"No, not a vacation. I'm taking the equivalent of a weekend."

"But what if— Fine." She released an exasperated breath. "If something comes up, tell the staff to call me. I'll figure out a way to handle it from here."

"They won't have to call you. If they need something, *I'll* handle it."

"And Chloe? Have you assigned someone to assist her while you're off?"

"That's handled, too." Not telling her about Chloe wasn't a lie of omission, it just wasn't her business.

"Well, I guess I just have to believe that it's handled."

Believe? The word started to burrow in and dig up frustration. He stopped it. "I'll talk to you when I get back. Bye, Zurie." He hung up.

Soon. Another key word. In a few weeks, she'd sign over what used to be his father's share of the ownership…and they'd have to come to an understanding.

But, right now, he didn't want to think about Zurie, the stable or the guesthouse.

He got out of the SUV and each step to the back door refueled anticipation in seeing Chloe.

Inside the cottage, he peeked into the laundry room. Her clothes hung on hangers lined up on a pole above the washer and dryer and on a drying rack in the corner. There weren't any piles of clothes on the floor or the machines. That was a good sign. Where was she?

In the kitchen, as he poured a glass of water from the pitcher in the fridge, the sound of running water behind a closed door in the vicinity of his bedroom confirmed she was in the bathroom.

Just as he was heading in that direction, someone knocked on the door. No one bothered him at the cottage except Zurie. Blake, Philippa and Gloria would call if they needed something.

Maybe one of the guests had gotten lost.

He crossed the living room and opened the door.

A model-thin brown-skinned woman with dark asymmetrically cut hair, wearing a short-sleeved emerald pantsuit and heels stood outside, looking over her shoulder. She faced Tristan, peering at him over large dark sunglasses.

His eyes had to be deceiving him.

Erica's crimsoned colored mouth curved upward with a self-assured smile. "Hello, Tristan."

Chapter Twenty-Two

Before Tristan could get past the shock, Erica walked inside. "It's so nice and cool in here after that long walk from the guesthouse." As she spun around to look at him the chain shoulder strap on her beige purse jangled. "I was surprised to see that the house isn't there anymore."

What the...? Forceful expletives ricocheted through his mind. It took everything within him not to take her by the arm and throw her back out. But she didn't just show up for no reason. What did she want?

Curiosity and suspicion overrode irritation. He slammed the door shut. "You don't care what happened to the house. You told the attorneys you couldn't wait to unload this place when you sold your ownership to Zurie."

"Of course, I have feelings for this place." Erica took off her glasses and gave him a wounded expression she'd probably practiced a thousand times. "This used to be my home."

"Used to be. You don't belong here now."

"I get it. You're upset. Jacob writing you out of his will must have been a complete shock. But you know that wasn't my fault. I felt terrible about it."

Those acting lessons she'd taken hadn't gone completely to waste. A harsh laugh escaped him. "Of course you did. You felt so bad about it that you wouldn't sell me the ownership you inherited in Tillbridge."

He'd sold most of his possessions, including the two horses he'd owned at the time, and taken out a loan to raise the cash to buy back his father's ownership. He'd even competed injured in a bull riding event for the prize money. And when he'd made her a fair offer, she'd refused it.

"I feel terrible about that, too. I'm here to make amends." She walked away from him and placed her things on the coffee table. When she turned back around, her mouth trembled. "But you have to understand. I was in pain over losing Jacob."

"You were in pain?" A vision of his father lying in his hospital room alone emerged and anger came with it. "After his stroke, he needed you. Did you even care about what happened to him?"

"We had already agreed to separate."

"No. You walked out on him."

"So did you." Her obstinate expression dared him to deny it.

"You know why I left. Did you honestly believe I would sleep with you? You were my father's wife." A position he'd put Erica in. He'd all but served his father up to this selfish woman when he'd brought her to Tillbridge. "He really loved you. You knew you didn't feel the same. There were wealthier men out there. Why marry him?"

"I didn't have a choice." She wrapped her arms around herself and her brown-eyed gaze dropped to the floor. Shame? Regret? It was the first real reaction he'd ever gotten from her. But when she looked back up, the vulnerability he'd glimpsed was gone. She dropped her arms to her sides and advanced toward him. "Don't you dare stand there and judge me. I was broke, and in debt and I had nowhere else to go. He gave me a way out, and I took it. Maybe I wouldn't have if you would have been here instead."

"And what was I supposed to be? Your consolation prize or some kind of upgrade? Forget it. I don't want to know. So unless you have a good reason for taking up my time, you need to leave."

She marched to her large bag and took something out wrapped in a blue cloth.

When she came back to him, it took a minute for him to register what the tarnished metal object was that she held out to him. It was the prize buckle from the Father's Day Rodeo. His dad had actually kept it?

A rush of nostalgia almost tempted him to take it. "You're not just handing it over to me. How much do you want?"

Anger entered her eyes. "Do you want to know why I wouldn't sell you my ownership in the stables?"

"No because it doesn't matter anymore."

"From the moment you sat next to me on the plane, you thought you were better than me. Well, I'm just not some charity case you brought to the family cookout. I have the same last name you think is so precious tacked onto mine, but you seem to forget that." She cocked her head. "You know, I came here planning to sell you this at a decent price, but forget it. I'm done with the Tillbridges. I'll just take this and the photos I found elsewhere."

Erica turned and stuffed the buckle into her bag. As she started to walk out, she remembered her sunglasses that she'd left on the coffee table and went back for them.

What would she do now? Sell the buckle to some random collector?

The image of his father, lying in the hospital came back up in his mind. No. Jacob Tillbridge wasn't a weak, broken man. He'd lived out his dreams competing in rodeos. He'd built Tillbridge Stable out of the dust with tenacity and determination. He'd provided him a home and raised him in the best way he'd known how.

She walked past him, sunglasses on.

He wasn't going to let her sell his father's memories to the highest bidder and toss what she couldn't make a profit from like trash. "Erica, wait."

She faced him and took off her glasses. A hint of smugness was in her expression.

Just as he was about to give her a dollar amount, something illuminated in his mind. He'd read every line of the offer his attorney had drawn up to buy back his father's ownership in Tillbridge from Erica. One part of it, in particular, stood out to him now.

"Leave the buckle. And I expect you to send the photos and any other memorabilia you had that belonged to my father immediately."

"Excuse me?"

"You heard me." He walked over to her. "I'm pretty sure Zurie's offer had the same terms as the one my attorney presented to you. It encompassed the shares for Tillbridge *and* all of my father's memorabilia including his buckles, collections and photos."

Her confidence slipped for only a second but he caught it.

She shook her head. "I never said I had any of that."

The sound of high heels tapping on the floor made him and Erica glance over his shoulder.

Chloe stood at the beginning of the hallway.

He'd been so busy sparring with Erica he'd forgotten she was there.

As Chloe walked toward them, the cream shirt tucked loosely into the waist of her jeans billowed slightly. "I'm afraid you did say that."

Erica gave Chloe an up-and-down look. "Who are you?"

Chloe flashed a serene, confident smile. "I'm Tristan's attorney."

Chapter Twenty-Three

"You're his lawyer?" Erica looked to Tristan and then back to Chloe. "But you're not the one who made me the offer."

"Mr. Tillbridge has changed representation since then. I'm his new lawyer." Chloe held her head high, willing herself to exude confidence.

Earlier, she'd walked out of the bathroom and heard him talking to a woman. She didn't recognize her voice, but the tone in his hadn't been welcoming. She'd been packing as the conversation had grown heated, then she'd crept down the hall barefoot wanting to make sure Tristan was okay.

They'd been too close to the front door for her to see them, but after hearing Jacob's possessions mentioned, she'd figured out the woman was Erica. Remembering Philippa had called his stepmom a gold digger had prompted her to listen a little longer and take her phone out of her back jeans pocket, and hit Record.

She hadn't decided who to be until just a few seconds ago, when she'd left her phone behind, quickly changed into the linen shirt and grabbed the shoes.

Chloe stared at Erica, focusing on channeling the part of a legal genius, and hoped Tristan would play along. "So if I'm understanding correctly, you have possessions that belong to my client and you'd like to return them?"

"No, I have a prize belt buckle that I thought might have sentimental value to Tristan that I happened to find in storage. I just came by to give it to him."

"Oh?" Chloe feigned confusion. "I'm pretty sure you said you had photos, which I'm taking to mean souvenirs, or keepsakes of monetary or personal value. Is that how you took it?"

As she glanced at Tristan, what she saw in his eyes reminded her of what he'd said the night of their friendly dart game with Mace and Adam. *Hope you can back your play, Ace.*

She could. If it meant getting that prize buckle and the photos from Erica and wiping that haughty look from her face.

He crossed his arms over his chest and focused on Erica. "That's how I understood it. My father not only collected vintage prize buckles but rare photos, as well."

Erica shook her head and fidgeted in place. "No. That's not what I said. I turned everything over when we closed the sale. You heard it wrong."

"Oh." Chloe held up her phone. "Should I play what I recorded back to refresh your memory? Or should I just save it for when we take you to civil court. I'm sure a judge would be interested in hearing *everything* you said to my client as well as revisiting any legal papers you signed regarding possessions in the ownership transfer."

Erica visibly swallowed. "I have nothing to say to you."

"That sounds like a wise move. In the meantime, we'll take that prize buckle you brought with you. You're so right about the sentimental value, not to mention it belongs with the rest of the collection."

Erica looked as if she was on the verge of an angry cry as she reached into her purse and handed the buckle to her.

"Thank you so much for dropping it off. We'll be in touch." Chloe flashed her best saccharine sweet smile and wiggled her phone in the air.

Erica opened her mouth as if to protest, but shut it, staring at Chloe's phone. She turned and stalked out, leaving the door open.

Tristan shut it behind her.

Chloe exhaled in relief. It worked. Erica was gone and Tristan had the prize buckle.

Tristan stood with his back to her at the door.

What was he thinking? Was he upset? "Are you okay?" she asked.

"I didn't know you'd studied law." His low even tone made her slightly anxious.

"I haven't. But, I did study lawyers in a court room.

I played the role of an attorney once in a show. It wasn't a big part or anything, but I really wanted to get the tone right. You know me, always be prepared." The absurdity of what she'd just said in comparison to what she'd just done struck her all at once.

The triumph of driving Erica from the cottage and getting the buckle from her was replaced by uncertainty and mounting dread. Was he mad about her impromptu performance?

Chloe took a tentative step toward him. She held up the buckle in her hand. "When I heard all the things she said to you and then she was dangling this prize buckle in front of you, it upset me."

"So you decided to wade in and pretend to be a lawyer?"

"I felt I had to do something. Like she said, this is rightfully yours." Chloe laid the buckle on the coffee table. "I'm sorry, maybe I was wrong for jumping into the middle of the conversation, but I couldn't just stand by and let her leave with it."

Tristan turned and walked over to her wearing an unreadable expression.

But by doing something, had she done the wrong thing? Chloe swallowed against the tightness in her throat and stared down at her feet. She'd just wanted to help but maybe all she'd done was butt in. After all, she didn't know the whole story about their history. She'd just assumed based on what she'd picked up from Rina and Philippa that day at brunch.

Chloe lifted her head, and just as she went to apologize, a slow smile came over his mouth. "You were amazing."

Her legs weakened with her relief as he kissed her hard and brief. "So you're not mad at me for barging in?"

"Are you serious? No." He held her in a loose embrace. "Of all my father's prize buckles that one means the most to me. We won it together in a team calf roping competition." He glanced at the buckle on the table, then looked into her eyes. "That was the first and only time we'd ever done something like that together. It was a good day for us. I didn't think I'd ever see it again. But you helped me get it back."

He kissed her, and her world spun in the warmth of happiness and desire. She wrapped her arms around him and leaned in to it.

A long moment later, they eased out of the kiss but not from each other.

He leaned his forehead to hers and she caressed his nape. "Maybe we should leave before someone else shows up on your doorstep."

"We should talk first."

His serious tone caused a sinking feeling to drop inside of her. "About?"

"Me and Erica."

Tristan closed his eyes. Meeting Erica on the plane. Taking her to his family's cookout. Erica trying to sleep with him. The last thing he wanted to do was talk about that, but Chloe had overheard a conversation that without the proper explanation could be misunderstood.

He took her hand and led her toward the couch.

She lagged behind him. "You don't have to explain anything to me."

"I know. But I want you to know the truth." He didn't want any lingering questions or doubts on her end possibly spoiling their short getaway.

She laid her phone on the coffee table next to the prize buckle. After they sat down, she smiled and said, "Okay. I'm listening." But her hand was stiff as he kept his fingers intertwined with hers.

He met her gaze. "First off, Erica was never my girlfriend. We never even dated."

Chloe's shoulders dropped with a deep exhale. "Oh, I'm so glad." Her relief morphed to exasperation and she punched his arm. "Why didn't you lead with that instead of the whole ominous 'we should to talk' intro? I thought I was going to have to do some major incense burning, 'woosah,' mind cleansing to erase the image of you two together."

"Yeah, I probably should have led with a version of that."

"You really don't have to explain anything. I got an unintentional heads-up about her from Philippa when we were at Rina's place for brunch. She called her a gold digger. And when a wedding photo of Erica and your father slipped out of one of Rina's photo albums, her reaction pretty much confirmed there was a problem with her."

An image of the day Erica and his father got married flashed through his mind. He'd tried to remain optimistic. His father had looked so happy, but even then, he didn't have a good feeling about what was ahead.

"I want to tell you." As he sat back on the couch, Chloe slipped off her shoes. She curled her leg under her and turned toward him. He took a deep breath. "This is the short version of how Erica and I met four and a half years ago—I was sitting next to her on a plane when I was flying home for Memorial Day weekend. Erica got ditched at the airport by a friend. She had very little money, no one to call and no place to go. I couldn't just leave her stranded. So I found her a hotel room, paid for it, and brought her here that Saturday afternoon to celebrate the holiday with me and my family."

"That was a sweet thing to do."

"I made a mistake."

"No." She squeezed his hand. "Don't say that. Yes, it was terrible how things unfolded, but calling what you did a mistake is the same as saying what unfolded after that with her and your father was your fault. It wasn't."

The conviction in her eyes almost made him believe it. "I should have protected my father from her. When she found out we owned the stable, I practically saw dollar signs in her eyes. After I made it clear to her that I wasn't interested, I noticed her being overly friendly with him, but I blew it off. I never dreamed she'd contact him after I left. I also could have told him my concerns before he married her, but I smiled and went along with it. And the night I walked out of the shower and found her in my bed, I should have walked straight to his room and told him about it. But I just kicked her out and waited until the next morning. By then she'd already put her spin on things."

Chloe's brow rose. "So she told your father that you tried to sleep with her?"

"Not exactly. She'd cried to him about how I was mistreating her, and not welcoming her into the family. And that I would do or say anything to sabotage their marriage. That led to his ultimatum. Either I left or he would with Erica. That would have devastated Zurie and Rina. He was the last tie to their father. And he still had so much to teach Zurie about running this place. Their well-being and the running of the stable was important—they all needed him more than they needed me."

"But…" Chloe shook her head in disbelief. She laid a hand on his thigh. "And Rina and Zurie just let you go?"

Echoes of the same disappointment and sadness that had burned into him then struck now. And just like when he'd looked into his father's eyes and saw he meant it, his words dried up. He couldn't answer her question. He didn't have to.

Realization slowly came over her face. "You didn't tell them what happened. You just left. That's when you started bull riding again. Isn't it?"

"Among other things. Aside from amateur bull riding, I also worked at a couple of horse farms training horses."

Chloe's unhappy expression made him sit up and scoot closer to her. "Everything turned out okay."

"But she cost you your relationship with your father, and I heard Erica say you were disinherited."

"I was. But my father and I reconciled before he died, and I'm getting my father's share of the stable back that Zurie bought from Erica. Now, I'll have the rest of his memorabilia, thanks to you."

She gave him a rueful smile. "If I would have known all of this when she was here, I would have squeezed a little more out of her. She should be made to pay you for your father's things like she should have in the first place. Even that's not nearly enough for what she put you through and then she had the nerve to come here."

"It's enough for now. What you did was one of the bravest, best things that anyone has ever done for me."

"I'm just glad I could help." Chloe glanced at her phone on the coffee table. "I'll share the recording with you. I hope it came out clear enough so your real attorney can use it." She looked back at him. "You're going to tell Rina and Zurie, too, right?"

A chance to shift the blame from himself to Erica? As tempting as that felt, it didn't make sense to do that now. Nothing could undo all that had happened. He and Zurie especially needed to find a way to bury the past and move forward.

"I'll figure that out when we get back. Let's start our weekend." Tristan stood and pulled Chloe to her feet.

In less than twenty, they were on the road. As they zipped by the stable his phone buzzed in the cup holder in the middle console.

Chloe glanced at it with a dejected expression, his

own heart plummeted until he remembered—"It's just an alarm to remind me to leave the office."

She released a breath and smiled. "You're early."

"I couldn't wait to see you." He reached across the console, took her hand and kissed it.

"Neither could I." She kept her hand were he put it on his thigh. "So, are you going to tell me where we're going now?"

Chapter Twenty-Four

After a long few seconds Tristan glanced over at her. "Nope."

Impatience laced with excitement pulled out a huff. She playfully swatted his thigh. "Oh, come on, the suspense is killing me."

Smiling, he kept his eyes on the road.

She looked for road signs but mostly stately homes set far back on a stretch of lawn or nestled in the trees surrounded them.

One sign finally came into view. I-95 10 miles.

She had him now. Kind of. If they went south, Baltimore, DC, or some place in Virginia were top picks. Virginia Beach maybe? He had told her to pack a swimsuit. The other day, she'd driven the next town over to Walmart and found a peach-colored monokini, along with a couple of pairs of jeans. She couldn't put on the one's she'd been wearing around the stable. They were worn looking, permanently stained, and faded from continuously having to wash them. But if they went north, Philadelphia was a possibility. New York, too.

Tristan blew past the right turn onto the road leading to the interstate on-ramp.

As she glanced back at it, he chuckled. "You'll never guess, so relax and enjoy the ride, we're almost there."

"Fine."

The scenery *was* pretty. Intermingled with the houses were pastures with cows and horses and farmland. So much green. If she were home right now, she'd be on the freeway battling traffic and exhaust fumes instead of enjoying this view. The same pang of sadness she'd felt at the cottage started to surface and she breathed it away.

A short time later, he turned right onto a gravel road that turned into a long paved one that cut through an expansive area of lush, trimmed grass bordered with trees. It led to a lone modern two-story with a double-pitched roof, beige brick and blue siding, and white trim.

The area. The house itself. They were both so beautiful she didn't know which to take in first. Was this Tristan's? But wasn't the cottage his home? "Who lives here?"

Tristan stopped the SUV several yards away. "I do. Or at least I will. The builders finished a few months ago. I'm still painting, installing fixtures and finalizing a few other details." He squeezed her hand. "But we don't have to stay here. If you'd rather go someplace else, it's not a problem."

"Of course I want to stay here. This place looks wonderful." She peered out the windshield, trying to get a better look of what lay behind the house.

"Are you sure this is fine?"

The slight hint of surprise in his voice made her ...ce at him. "Yes. Why wouldn't it be?"

"I thought maybe you'd prefer to be in a nice hotel in the city with restaurants and shops, and that sort of thing."

The sincerity in his eyes tugged at her heart. He really would drive back to the interstate and take her anywhere she wanted to go. She leaned over the console. "The only thing I prefer is you for as long as we can get away. And being able to spend time with you here—" she glanced at his home "—makes it even better." As she kissed him, his mouth curled upward.

He still had a smile on his face as he pulled the SUV to the side of the house and parked outside of the two-car garage.

They got out. As Tristan walked down a light stone path from the driveway to the front porch, carrying their bags, she followed.

She glanced around. It was definitely a peaceful spot away from the hustle and bustle of life. "So when's the last time you've been here?"

Tristan punched a code into the keypad above the door handle. "Two days ago. I stocked a few basics— bath towels, plates and other things we'd need, just in case we decided to stay." He went inside first and deactivated the alarm on the wall panel.

Chloe walked inside. Polished dark-wood flooring ran from the foyer and throughout what she could see of the first floor. The light smell of fresh paint from the cream-colored walls lingered with the pleasant fragrance of what reminded her of eucalyptus and lavender. While she slipped off her tennis shoes, Tristan set down their bags in the entryway and took off his boots.

They walked forward. Beige carpeted stairs ran up the right. An empty room sat on the left. High ceilings and lots of light coming in through the front and back windows gave the space a bright open feel.

"I love the floor plan. Lots of windows, not too many walls shutting out the light."

"That's what I was going for." As Tristan took her hand, he pointed to the empty room. "This is supposed to be a formal dining room, but I'm not sure that's what it's going to be."

A sitting room... That's what came to Chloe's mind. Plants and furniture with overstuffed cushions. If the window was facing east, the sunrise from that spot, or even the porch, would be spectacular. The perfect place to enjoy morning coffee and take in the view.

"There's an office space down here." He gestured to a hallway just off the right of the stairs. "And of course, the living room." Tristan pulled her forward into a large space with a midnight blue couch in the middle of it and a brown-and-beige stone fireplace with a flat screen television mounted above it.

It was easy to envision him sitting there with a plate

of food or a drink in hand watching a ball game. She smiled.

He looked over at her. "What?"

She glanced at the television. "Just admiring your decorating."

He offered up a shrug. "The only way I could get Mace out here to help me install some tile and the deck last month was with the promise of food and a way to watch footfall."

"Sure, blame it on Mace."

Tristan laughed. "Come on, let me show you the rest."

The back windows overlooked a deck with two Adirondack chairs, a grill and a covered area on the end with a hammock. Beyond that, another beautiful grassy landscape unfolded with something on it that didn't surprise her. An area circled by a white ladder fence and a nearby structure, most likely a small stable.

"Are you bringing Thunder here to live with you?"

"Maybe. But if he adapts to trail riding with the guests, I'll leave him at Tillbridge. Jett's owner is possibly looking to sell. But I'll wait until I can find another horse to keep him company before I bring him out. I also need to fence off an area for the them to graze. But me coming here to live isn't happening anytime soon."

It was a wonderful spot with so much room and a commutable distance from the stable. If she were him, she would have moved in right away. But that just showed how dedicated he was to Tillbridge. Not even his own home took precedence over the stable.

"How much land do you have?"

He led her toward the adjacent smaller dining area. "The property is nearly seven acres total, including the house."

The dining area led to the kitchen that boasted light wood cabinets, cream marble counters, an eight-burner built-in gas stove and drop-down lighting over a long marble-topped island separating it from the living room.

"I had the builder put in an island instead of a wall and add some extra storage." He pointed to a nice-sized space off to the side with shelving.

A large, walk-in pantry...a center island. That was Philippa's description of the kitchen in Tristan, Rina and Zurie's family home. Was he thinking of that space when he designed his?

Next, they grabbed their bags and went upstairs.

He pointed out the two guestrooms in the middle of the hall and the bonus room at the end. On the other end was the main bedroom.

It felt wrong to just walk in before of him. Chloe slowed down, but Tristan nudged her forward. "Go ahead."

Tristan hung back and let her look around. Just like the other rooms, it was sparsely furnished.

Chloe paused by the king-sized poster bed against the wall with round wood columns covered by a beige comforter and with rust and slate pillows propped near the headboard. "I love the color combination."

"Thanks." It was the same ensemble that had been on display at the store when he bought the bed. But there was no need to tell her that, just like she didn't need to know that she'd be the first to share this space with him intimately. Bringing her there was a big step but it didn't feel like a huge leap.

She wandered to the adjoining bathroom, and her squeal of delight wasn't a total surprise. "Oh, my gosh!"

He peeked over her shoulder at the dove-gray tiled, spa bathroom he'd installed with a large sunken tub in one corner and a glass-enclosed shower that took up the other. As Tristan stood behind her, he rested his hands on her waist. "I guess this meets your approval."

"Are you kidding? I could spend the rest of the day in here." She glanced at him and grinned. "Not that I don't want to spend time with you or anything."

"Uh-huh. Well, you may want to hold off on that decision." He led her past the bed to the tinted window that took up most of the wall above the far end of the deck she hadn't been able to see from where she stood downstairs. "Take a look."

Chloe peeked out and she released a blissful sigh. "Is that a hot tub?"

"Yes."

He'd added both tubs to the design of the house, imagining himself soaking away the aches and pains from his old injuries and decompressing from long days at the stable. But Chloe's response raised an eagerness to share both places with her.

Tristan pulled her loosely into his arms. "You can decide which one you want to get in first after we get back."

"From where?"

"The grocery store. I thought we could shop together so you can pick out the food you want while we're here. And we don't just have to hang around the house. There's a pick-your-own fruit and vegetable farm in the area. Strawberries are still in season. There's also a winery that isn't too far away and a chocolate factory with a restaurant that specializes in unique recipes that incorporate chocolate into their entrées."

"Wow. You're making this so hard to decide." She looped her arms around his neck. "Do I have to make up my mind now?"

"No. Just let me know what you want to do, and we'll do it." He kissed her. What was supposed to be one brief kiss turned into a long one that had them inching toward the bed.

But he halted their progress. "Food first. Otherwise, we won't go anywhere for the rest of the day, and then we'll starve." Her hand stroking his nape raised goose bumps and more temptation.

She laughed. "You're right. Let's go."

The drive to the local store that was a one-stop shop for gas, groceries, hardware and other miscellaneous supplies didn't take long. Shopping for food wasn't a chore as they both agreed on the basics they needed: eggs for breakfast along with the thick-cut bacon he liked, prepackaged salad for lunch or dinner and the ginger dressing she preferred. Steak and chicken for the grill along with a few vegetables.

They decided to stock up on strawberries and some other fresh produce at the farm. That would be their first excursion together in the morning, after that, maybe the restaurant for a late lunch or early dinner.

Just as they were heading out of the store to the parking lot, Chloe waved him ahead to the car and doubled back. Fifteen minutes later, she came out with a bag knotted shut.

As she got into the car. Tristan glanced at it. "Find what you needed?"

Chloe's smile held a bit of mischief. "Yes."

She remained protective of the bag, not allowing him to touch it, even when they got to the house. Chloe put the bag in a far corner of the pantry. "Promise me you won't look inside."

Tristan peeked at it over her shoulder. "Don't I even get a hint?"

"No." She patted his chest. "You're not the only one who can keep a surprise."

Soon, they busied themselves with dinner, teaming up on making grilled steak and potato salad.

Close to sunset, they found themselves in the hot tub.

As Tristan relaxed in the tub, he wrapped his arms around from behind Chloe as she sat between his legs. She looked so sexy in her bathing suit, he couldn't stop touching her even if he'd wanted to. Which he sure as hell didn't.

He let what little tension was left inside of him leave in the heated water swirling around him. Having Chloe there in his home, wrapped in his arms, watching the last of the sun slip below the horizon—with no place to go for the rest of the night but upstairs to his bed-room—felt more than right.

She laid her head back on his shoulder. "You know what."

"What?"

"This place." Chloe looked to the house. "Best va-cation spot ever. Seriously, you could Airbnb it if you wanted to if you're not moving in for a while."

Just a vacation spot? Nothing to do with them being in his home there together? A strange tinge of disap-pointment pinged inside of him, but he caught it and tossed it aside. He'd promised her a getaway, he'd taken her there and she was happy. That's all that mattered.

He kissed her. "Being here is a great getaway."

Chapter Twenty-Five

Tristan carried the short wide cardboard crate with berries into the kitchen. As he set it on the counter a few of the strawberries fell onto the tile floor.

Chloe quickly set her black paisley boho bag on the island, scooped them up and washed them off in the sink. She bit into one and juice dripped onto her sky blue T-shirt. Not that she cared. It was already smudged along with her jeans and tennis shoes from wading through rows of berry plants, searching for the best fruit to pick. And it was worth it.

He glanced at the fruit in her hand. "Can I have some or do you plan to eat all of those, too?"

Earlier they'd washed a few off before getting into the car to drive home, and she'd pretty much eaten them all.

Laughing, she held the largest one in her hand to him. Instead of taking it from her, he just bit into it. He suffered the same fate she had with berry juice landing on his T-shirt.

Tristan licked his lips and wiped his chin. "So you're serious about never having picked a fruit or vegetable from a plant?"

"Very. Not even leaves from an herb plant on my window sill. Well, actually someone did give me a basil plant once, but it didn't make it."

He shook his head and kissed her. "City girl, you have a lot to learn."

"Are you offering to teach me?" She grabbed the front of his shirt and pulled him in for another strawberry flavor–filled kiss.

Lena's pop song ringtone chimed from her phone in her bag.

The unexpected sound drew her attention as well as Tristan's.

"It's my agent." Still, she didn't move to answer it. She and Tristan had gone through almost a whole twenty-four hours without interruptions.

"You should get that." He kissed her cheek. "I'll get the rest of the stuff from the car."

Just before it flipped to voice mail, she answered. "Hey, Lena, what's up?"

"Changes. Lots and lots of changes."

Had she lost another part? Chloe's heart sank. "What do you mean?"

"Nash Moreland. Do you know him?"

Who didn't know him? Dirty blond hair, deep blue

eyes, a camera-ready smile, currently on everyone's sexiest man alive list, and as an actor, he was establishing himself in action films. But that's not what Lena meant about knowing him.

"We met through friends a few years ago before his career took off." She snagged more fruit from the crate and washed it off. "They even set us up on a blind date. Or is that called a surprise date since technically we knew each other?"

"Who cares what it was called, please just tell me you two ended whatever happened on a good note."

"We actually got along well. The only reason we didn't go out again was because he flew to Italy to make a movie. Right after that his film career started taking off, and we went our separate ways. Why?"

"Nash is taking over as the leading actor in Holland's film. The other guy, I can't remember his name right now, but he's out and Nash is in."

What *was* that guy's name? Chloe plucked the top from the strawberry in her hand and put the fruit in her mouth. But that was typical of Hollywood. The things you did either made you easy to remember or quickly forgotten.

Lena continued, "Nash has input on who's playing what parts in his films, including this one. He'll even be there for your audition. From what I hear, he really gets into playing his characters, this one included. He's at a horse farm as we speak so he'll be ready to ride at the auditions."

Chloe swallowed the strawberry prematurely. *Ready to ride?* She must have been hearing things. She actually thought she'd heard Lena say something about the auditions involving a horse. "You mean just Nash on a horse at the other auditions, not mine."

"No. You and him riding horses. The other thing that's happened, Holland is expanding the role you're auditioning for…"

Riding horses. This couldn't be happening.

"Isn't that great?" Lena's enthusiasm pulled Chloe back into the conversation. "Now aren't you glad that you've gotten all of that experience with horses?"

"Uh…yeah."

As Leah ended the call on a high note, dismay sank into Chloe's stomach along with the strawberry.

Tristan strolled into the kitchen carrying the combination crate of fresh carrots and peas. "Why don't w—" He looked to her and immediately set the crate on the counter. "What's wrong?"

Everything. This was not supposed to happen.

Concern grew in his face when she didn't answer him. He lightly grasped her shoulders. "What did Lena say?"

She met his gaze. "I'm doomed."

Chapter Twenty-Six

Chloe startled herself half awake. Several seconds later, she registered that she was lying in Tristan's bed at his house.

It was just a bad dream—riding and falling off a horse at her audition. In reality, she didn't have to ride a horse with…

Chloe opened her eyes. Sunlight and shadows patterned the ceiling. No. She really did have to audition on a horse with Nash Moreland…and she had to leave Maryland early.

She reached for Tristan and her hand rested on the cool empty sheet. When she'd told him the news, he'd been so supportive and reassuring that everything would be okay. Over dinner at the chocolate-themed restaurant, where she'd hardly eaten the coffee-and-chocolate-glazed short ribs she'd ordered, he'd assured her she could learn to ride in a week. Or at least stay upright and not fall off like in the dream she'd just had. Her heart started to pound as her past and the dream collided into something that felt very real in her mind. Why was this happening to her?

A longing for Tristan's solid warmth made her sit up in bed. She listened for sounds in the house. All was quiet. Chloe slipped out of bed, pulling down the hem of her pink STRESSED, BLESSED & CAFFEINE OBSSESSED sleep shirt as she went into the bathroom.

After taking care of the essentials, she walked downstairs.

Tristan's voice echoed from the short hallway on the right leading to what would become his home office.

She peeked in. He was at the far end of the room, drinking from a mug and talking on the phone in the empty space with light spilling in from a side window. He was already dressed in a white T-shirt that hugged his chest and a pair of jeans.

Just before she was about to duck out and give him privacy, Tristan met her gaze and tipped his head, motioning for her to come in. He met her halfway and as he talked on the phone, he loosely wrapped his free arm around her along with the mug.

"Yeah, that should work." As Tristan listened to the person on the line, he brushed a kiss near her temple.

She wrapped her arms around his waist and breathed him in along with the scent of coffee. Up close, near his jawline, he not only smelled like his soap, but something else was there that reminded her of wide open spaces under the sun.

"Okay. I think we're good to go," he said. "I'll take care of that now. Thanks. Bye." Tristan turned to look at her and his hazel-brown eyes focused on her face. "Good morning."

"Good morning." She lifted up slightly on her toes and kissed him.

"You were tossing and turning for most of the night. Did you get any sleep?"

"A little." Wanting to be near him, but unable to resist the pull of caffeine, she moved from his arms and slipped the coffee mug from his hand. It was sweeter than she usually drank it, but still good. "What time do you want to leave?"

"Are you in a hurry?" He took her free hand and stroked over her knuckles with his thumb.

Not even close. If she could have another day of escape, she'd be more than tempted to grab onto it. "No, but I know you have to get back to the stable. I'm sure they're calling you."

"I've got time." He said that, but he looked preoccupied. "Are you okay here by yourself for an hour or so? I need to make a run to the store."

"I'll be fine."

"Need anything?"

"No, I'm good." He gave her hand a light squeeze and walked out of the room.

Moments later, the front door opened, then she heard the faint rumbling of a car engine.

She wandered through the downstairs, sipping coffee. The caffeine started to erase the foggy feeling in her head, allowing her to appreciate the smooth coolness of the wood floor beneath her feet, the natural light adding a layer of vibrancy, and how the lack of furniture made the rooms even more open and inviting.

I could get used to this...

As she stood in the front room, looking out at the lawn, a vision came to mind of a different start to her day—this time, waking up with Tristan.

They'd both be reluctant to leave each other to begin their day. She'd nestle further into his arms, his chest the perfect pillow, his heartbeat tempting her to fall back to sleep. But then they'd get up, tag team turns in the shower and in front of the bathroom mirror, get dressed and then go to the kitchen for mugs of steaming coffee. He'd go to Tillbridge, and depending on the task at hand, she'd either hang in the back office talking to Lena about her next big acting or directing project; or maybe she'd camp out where she was now standing—it definitely wouldn't be a formal dining room, but just as she'd envisioned it when she first walked into the house. And if it was too beautiful a day to miss, she'd curl up in his hammock out back.

But that was just a daydream. An illusion to preoccupy her so she wouldn't have to face what was next. Leaving the house. Leaving Tillbridge. Her audition in LA. Riding a dang horse with Nash who was probably a horse whisperer by now. That was her reality.

After washing her mug out in the sink, she went into the pantry to find the oatmeal. The bag she made

Tristan promise not to open caught her eye. It contained her thank-you to him for their getaway.

Chloe took it to the kitchen and unpacked the lemon poppy seed muffin mix, powdered sugar and a red silicone muffin pan on the counter. She grabbed the rest of the ingredients needed—butter, milk, eggs and fresh lemons—from the refrigerator.

Not much of a baker, but knowing that lemon was Tristan's favorite flavor, she'd wanted to make something special for him. She'd reached out to Rina for help with a lemon pie, what she thought was his favorite dessert, but Rina told her it wasn't. His all-time favorite lemony treat was actually lemon poppy seed muffins. Rather than tackle baking them from scratch, Rina had given the name of a brand that made a mix that wasn't as good as her homemade muffins, of course, but passable. Especially with the homemade glaze.

Chloe turned on the oven, then rummaged around the cabinets and drawers until she found the bowls and utensils she needed. Following the instructions, she made the mix, spooned the batter into the pan and put it in the oven.

She made note of the time. Hopefully, Tristan would be gone closer to an hour so she could get everything done. Picking up the pace, she squeezed lemons in a bowl with the sugar and mixed it together. Unable to resist, she licked the spoon. Tart and sweet, and so easy to make—she liked it. Chloe ate another spoonful before cleaning up and washing the dishes. By the time she finished, the muffins were done. She drank more coffee, and ate more glaze than she probably should have, waiting for them to cool. Then just like Rina had instructed her, she spooned on the glaze while they were still slightly warm. The dozen golden muffins glistened on the plate. They looked good, but how did they taste?

A car engine echoed.

Instead of coming through the front door, Tristan came in through the side door next to the garage that led into the laundry room just off the kitchen.

Not wanting to give away her surprise yet, on a reflex she stuck the plate in an empty cabinet above her.

Tristan walked into the kitchen.

"Hey." She smiled brightly, feeling all kinds of guilty.

He sniffed the air and gave her a quizzical look. "Did you bake something?" His gaze landed on the muffin pan. "Did you make cupcakes?"

"No, not quite." She backed up and leaned against the counter. "Just a little something."

"So what is it? I smell lemons." Humor was in his eyes as he walked over to her. "Come on, tell me." Tristan leaned in as if to kiss her and paused.

As he reached behind her, she realized what he was going for. The glaze. She'd left it out.

He took the spoon out of it and as he licked it, a curious expression came over his face. "Did you make me lemon poppy seed muffins?"

She pointed up and behind her. "See for yourself."

Tristan opened the cabinet and grinned. She moved aside so he could take them down and put them on the counter. "This is what you were hiding from me at the store?" He picked one up and grinned. "Who told you these were my favorites? Rina?"

"Yes." She couldn't stop herself from grinning back at him. "I saw some lemon cookies and a tart way back on the bottom shelf in the bakery. You'd missed them. But when I called her about which one to buy, she said you liked the muffins more."

"Thank you." He gave her a long, lingering kiss that had her leaning into him.

"Don't thank me yet. You haven't tasted them."

The sound of a car engine grew louder as it came from the back of the house.

She looked to Tristan. "You have contractors here today?"

"Not contractors." He took her hand. "Come take a look." Tristan led her from the kitchen to the adjoining space near the living room with a view of the back.

Adam and another groom were unloading Moonlight Joy from a horse trailer.

Tristan stood beside her and wrapped an arm around her waist.

"Is that where you went, back to the stable, to bring her here for me?" Suddenly overcome by tears, she turned and burrowed her face into his shoulder.

He held her close. "I actually did go to the store for hardware for the stall out back. But I called Adam to bring her. I thought it might be less intimidating if you had your first lesson here without people around. You can take as much time as you need today to ease into it."

She took in a shaky breath and inhaled his wonderful scent, and just like her first day at the stable it and his strength reassured her. "Can you really spare Adam for the day?"

"He's not teaching you. I am. They're just dropping off Moonlight, then they're heading back."

She looked into his eyes. "Really? Can you do that?"

He quirked a brow. "Do what? Teach you how to ride a horse? Do I need to show you my résumé or something?"

"You know what I mean." She poked him in the stomach and he chuckled.

He kissed her forehead. "Yeah, I got time. It's important." Tristan looked sincerely into her eyes. "You're important."

Less than an hour later, Chloe was dressed in a lime T-shirt, jeans and her cowboy boots, gripping the reins and trying to stay balanced on Moonlight in the arena. She hazarded a look down at Tristan, standing beside her. "I thought you said I had all day to ease into this?"

He held on to the bridle as Moonlight settled in place. Despite his serious expression, hints of amusement were in his eyes as he looked up at her. "This is easing into it. What did you think we were going to do?"

"I don't know. Talk me through it first."

"You need to leave in a few days for your audition. What do you think we should be doing right now? Talking about riding or riding? You tell me."

She flew home next Monday. The audition was soon after that. It really was that soon. Anxiety and dread intertwined and twisted into knots in her stomach. He was right. Talking about riding wasn't going to help her now. She had to learn to ride a horse, and feel as comfortable as possible doing it, if she wanted that part. And she did.

Chloe released a long shaky breath. "Okay. What do I need to do?"

"First, relax. Moonlight isn't going anywhere until we tell her to."

Moonlight fidgeted and Chloe clenched the reins.

Tristan reached up and squeezed Chloe's hand. "The only reason she's moving around is to coax you into the right position on the saddle. You're leaning back a little too much. That's making you feel off balance and causing you to pull too much on the reins. Find your seat. Think of being plugged into the saddle while there's a string from the top of your head pulling you up and keeping you straight."

Easy for him to say. His feet were firmly on the ground and not dangling high up. But what had Blake mentioned to her a while back? That if the rider was off balance, the horse would be, too. He'd also said that bad rider positioning and yanking on the reins could be painful for a horse. The last thing she wanted to do was hurt Moonlight.

Chloe adjusted her hips until she felt more comfortable in the saddle.

"Good. That's it. Sit tall and straight and just let your legs hang down naturally." He touched her calf, and the faint pressure of his hand through her jeans and boots was comforting. It also made her mind wander to last night, and how his caresses had felt on her skin.

"You're tensing up again."

No kidding. It was hard to relax when all she really wanted to do was go upstairs and get back in bed with him.

"Good. That's better. Now you're ready. I'm going to hold on to the lead rope for now. It's clipped to the side of the bit so she's not going anywhere we don't want her to go. We're just going to walk around the arena. You're okay. Now tell Moonlight you want her to move forward." He took his hand from her leg and stepped back.

The loss of his proximity made her heart pound and her mouth dry out, but she managed to make the clicking sound with her tongue against her teeth.

Moonlight walked forward at a slow, easy pace and Chloe rocked slightly in the saddle. Every part of her wanted to pull hard on the reins, but Chloe resisted, focusing on taking complete breaths so she wouldn't pass out.

But her life was in the hands of a horse who could decide to bolt at any moment to chase a bird or a squirrel, leaving her hanging on for dear life! Okay, maybe horses didn't chase things like dogs and cats, but they still had minds of their own. In fact, who knew what they were thinking? What was she thinking by letting Tristan talk her into the saddle?

She focused on him, just ahead of her and off to the side, the end of the slack lead rope in his hand. Or more accurately, she focused on the way his shirt molded to his shoulders and back and his jeans to his taut butt. The way he looked, he could talk her into pretty much anything.

Absorbed in the view, she almost missed it when Tristan told her to stop Moonlight near the end of the arena. He then talked her through using the reins and her legs to cue Moonlight to make turns.

The first left turn, Chloe couldn't stop her hands or legs from shaking. She tugged back on the reins confusing Moonlight, who took that as the sign to stop. Chloe felt as if she were about to fall.

"Chloe, you're fine. Balance your weight in the stirrups." Tristan spoke to her in the same soothing tones she'd witnessed him using on the horses. She would have been irritated but it worked.

On the second try, she managed to coordinate her hold on the reins and gently push with her foot and Moonlight made the turn.

"Not bad. Now tell her to stop."

"Whoa, Moonlight."

The horse coming to a stop raised a hint of confidence in Chloe. Maybe Moonlight wouldn't run off and not listen to her.

Tristan unclipped the lead rope. "Now walk her down to the other end and keep going around so you can practice turning."

"You want me to go that far…on my own?" The end of the arena seemed like it was a million miles away.

"You can do it, and I'll be right here. I'm not going anywhere. I got you."

His reassuring smile and the lack of worry in his eyes melted away more of her anxiety. Tristan wouldn't let her get hurt. After taking a long breath, Chloe clicked her tongue and Moonlight moved forward and he walked with them.

He glanced over at her. "What happened to make you so afraid of horses?"

"You want to know that now that I'm up here? Wouldn't that have been a good question to ask before I got up here?"

"Settle down. It's okay." Was he talking to her or Moonlight? "Now is the perfect time for you to talk about it. Moonlight probably needs to hear the reason so she can understand."

That was silly, of course. Moonlight couldn't decipher what she was saying.

Still, she released a deep breath as her mind went back in time. "When I was eleven, I convinced my mom to sign me up for a creative arts summer camp. My dad wasn't happy about it at all. He thought it was a waste of money and I should have been going to math camp. Anyway, we had to participate in an outdoor activity every morning before we did the creative stuff. On day two, the choices were horseback riding, canoeing or miniature golf."

"Ahh, now I get it. A horse followed you around in your canoe, and that's why you're afraid of horses. That makes perfect sense."

"Ha ha, aren't you the hilarious one?" But his silly joke made her smile. "If you're going to poke fun, I'll keep my compelling, drama-filled story of preteen angst to myself."

"Wouldn't miss it. I'm listening."

"Well, obviously, I chose horse riding. Not because I was interested in horses, but there was a boy named Todd."

"You got on a horse for a boy?"

"Don't knock it. I'm up here because of you."

He huffed a chuckle. "Good point. Keep going."

"So, I'd noticed him when I first got there, but he hadn't noticed me. I thought if I got on a horse…"

"You'd get his attention. And did you?'

"Yeah, but for all the wrong reasons." Chloe brought Moonlight to a standstill. "We were outside the front of the barn with the riding instructor. I volunteered to be the one to help him demonstrate how to sit on a horse. A few of the boys were rowdy and the instructor pulled them aside. One of the teen camp counselors was supposed to be holding on to the horse I was on, but he was more interested in making eyes at his girlfriend who was also a camp counselor. Apparently, someone spotted a wasp's nest and decided to poke it with a stick. The wasps got angry, people started running and screaming, and the horse got spooked and bolted."

Moonlight shifted around sparking memories of how the horse that day at camp had suddenly taken off down the path from the barn. Too frightened to scream as the horse jostled her, she'd tried desperately to hold on to the reins, but she couldn't. In the present, Chloe could feel the echoes of that fear climbing through her chest.

Tristan stroked up and down her thigh, soothing her through the memory.

She cleared her throat and her gaze dropped to the

reins in her hands. "I fell into a stack of hay bales on the side of the path. They cushioned my fall, but I ended up breaking my arm."

Tristan squeezed her leg. "Did you go back to camp?"

"No." A sad, quiet laugh slipped out. "My dad thought the accident proved that going there was a mistake. He didn't want me to go back and my mom was so upset about me getting hurt she agreed."

"So you never got a chance to move past your fear." Tristan looked down as he scuffed his boot on the ground. "As well as a few other things."

No. She was pretty sure her fear had to do with turning her life over to a creature with impulsive tendencies. But still... "Like what?"

"Trusting yourself." He looked up at her. "I'm sure your parents meant well, but I think not letting you go back to that camp and face your fear, and maybe even try riding a horse again, made you believe that falling off the horse was your fault."

"But it was. I made the stupid decision back then to ride one without understanding everything I needed to know."

"Not a stupid decision. Just *a* decision and in the midst of the experience you fell off a horse. And as far as learning everything you need to know, even experienced riders fall off horses. Lack of understanding isn't what's going to stop you from riding well. You walked away from it physically, but mentally..." He tapped his temple. "You're still there, judging yourself."

She opened her mouth, prepared to deny it, but she hesitated, remembering what her dad had told her back then.

People will feel sorry for you now because you got hurt, but all they'll remember in the future is how you fell off...

But today, "people" weren't remembering and judging what had happened to her...only she was.

"Let's give your legs a rest." Tristan motioned for her to get down and he held on to Moonlight's bridle as she swung her leg over the saddle and dismounted.

As she faced him, he rested his hands on her waist. "If you want this part you're auditioning for, Ace, it isn't about mastering how to ride a horse, you need to trust yourself and your decisions while doing it. You told me once that your parents and your brother are amazing at what they do." His gaze held hers. "You're no less amazing in what you do. Believe that."

Tristan continued with Chloe's lesson, making sure to take frequent breaks to give her legs and Moonlight a break. Late in the afternoon, they stopped for the day. After grooming Moonlight and getting her settled in a stall in the small stable, they went in through a side door next to the garage that led straight into what would be the laundry room once he got the washer and dryer installed.

Chloe leaned against the wall, struggling to remove her boots.

Tristan went over to her. "Let me help." He bent over and as she grasped his shoulder for balance, he tugged off one then the other. "You accomplished a lot today. You did well."

"Thank you." She sagged against the wall. Undoubtedly, she was stiff and sore.

"Want some help?"

She gave him a weary smile. "I think I can make it."

The laundry room opened to the kitchen. After drinking a glass of cool water, she started walking toward the stairs, but every other step Chloe winced. She wouldn't make it up to the second floor, at least not anytime soon.

"Come on." He swept her up in his arms and carried her up to the bedroom.

She nuzzled her face into his neck. "Are you going to take advantage of me?"

"I could, but I think a long soak in the tub might hold your attention more than I could right now."

"Not if you were wearing your Stetson."

The low, sexy tone of her voice made him look twice at her face.

"My Stetson? Why?"

She kissed his neck and he almost stumbled as he reached the landing. "Because you look so darn sexy in it."

If he would have known that he would have packed it first. As he set her down in the bedroom, she winced again as she stood straight. As much as he'd love to follow through on her Stetson fantasy, she needed the tub more.

He led her toward the bathroom where he planned to fill up the tub for her. "Since I don't have it with me, I'll see what I can come up with to hold your attention."

Chloe definitely liked his idea.

After a long soak in the tub, she lay front down on the bed. As she rested her head on her folded arms, he massaged her tired muscles, and she moaned in pleasure and relief. He'd mixed together a concoction of oils using the jojoba and lavender-scented oils she used in her facial routine with virgin olive oil.

"Feel good?" He kneaded the top of her right thigh.

Under any other circumstances, touching her would have raised desire, but the loosening of her knotted muscles and the way she melted under his touch satisfied him more.

"Better than good." She sighed. "Did you get a lot of massages when you were bull riding?"

He moved down her thigh to her calf. "Every now and then." Honestly, the majority of the time, he'd just iced up and taped up. Massages were a luxury he didn't have time for.

"Do you miss it?"

"Massages?"

"Very funny. No, competing."

He hesitated, letting the multiple rodeos he'd been in roll through his mind. "Yeah, there are days when I do, especially the camaraderie with the other riders." He huffed a chuckle. "But my body doesn't—that's my past. Making Tillbridge the best that it can be— that's my future."

Her eyes drooped shut and her breathing steadied.

Careful not to wake her, he covered her up with the sheet and comforter, then crept from the room.

Downstairs, he grabbed the second-to-last lemon poppy seed muffin from the plate. He'd been snacking on them all day and had eaten most of them, along with the glaze.

Bypassing the hammock he opted to sit in one of Adirondack chairs to take in the peacefulness of the early night while enjoying the last of the surprise Chloe had made for him. Did she have any idea what the muffins meant to him? Rina definitely did, but it didn't seem that she'd told Chloe.

As he finished and sucked the glaze off his thumb, time turned back to when Aunt Cherie made lemon poppy seed muffins for him and his father because they enjoyed them. But she had to bake them when he and his father weren't around, and hide them in the kitchen, so he and his father wouldn't eat them all before anyone else had a chance to get some. But the extra glaze she'd tuck away in the back of the fridge always gave it away. If he or his father spotted it, they immediately knew to start hunting around and whoever found them first, he or his father, would let the other know. And the amount of glaze they used to put on them was all kinds of wrong. They had to use bowls to eat the muffins because they were soaked with it.

As soon as he'd tasted the glaze Chloe had made and found the muffins, he'd honestly just wanted to kiss her, and keep kissing her. To take her upstairs to his bedroom and show her how much he'd appreciated what she'd done for him. He didn't have the words.

He didn't know how to explain to Chloe how easy it was to be with her, laugh with her, talk with her about everything including some difficult things from his past. Or what it had felt like those past few days, there at his home, to wake up and see her sleeping next to him. Or what he'd felt, being the one to teach her to ride a horse and watch her little by little, as the day went on, conquer her fear.

The rightness of having her there, along with all he couldn't put into words actually scared him a little, but it also made him happy in a way he hadn't felt since... He couldn't remember it had been so long.

He released a deep breath, and sank back in the chair. But rightness didn't change the facts. Like she'd said, being there with him for her was like a vacation. Chloe had a life to get back to...and it didn't include him.

Chapter Twenty-Seven

Chloe walked from the guesthouse to the stable. As her black boots landed solidly on the gravel trail, birds chirped, welcoming the sun inching up over the horizon. A morning breeze stirred the smells of rich green pasture, fresh hay and the faint smell of…horse manure. Funny. She was actually used to it now, just before it was time to leave. She was heading for the airport in Baltimore in a few hours to catch a plane to LA…and away from Tristan. But she'd promised to meet him at the stable one last time.

Since being at his home, they'd tried to make the most of the time they had left in between her continuing her riding lessons and his busy schedule.

Whenever she caught a glimpse of him during the day, they had traded smiles, or when no one was watching he'd wink at her, and she'd smile even more knowing the day would end with them being together. But last night, she just couldn't imagine resting her head on his chest, listening to his solid, steady heartbeat, and not cry her eyes out. Having to return to California early was taking away the time she'd planned on and needed to reconcile in her head and her heart about leaving Tristan.

After the surprise party the staff had thrown for her at the stable, she'd told him she couldn't spend the night with him because she needed to pack. Instead, she'd spent the majority of that time soaking in the tub and lying in bed awake, wielding the sharp edges of reality to cut the invisible yet tangible tie she felt to him. She couldn't let herself fall for him. Her life was in California and her next job could be anywhere. Tristan was just about to get back what mattered to him the most. Tillbridge. And the running of it along with the expansion he couldn't wait to implement would take up his attention as it should.

Chloe reached the intersection with the path leading from the stable to the arena.

Tristan waited for her outside the stable. He had on his Stetson. Her heart tripped. He never wore it around the stable. He'd clearly done it to please her, like taking her away, teaching her how to ride a horse, massaging her aches and pains away…and all of the little things he'd done for her lately, like letting her eat the last of the strawberries they'd picked or remembering to grab the extra blanket from the closet when they'd curled up on the couch to watch TV. And how he supported her and encouraged her without hesitation. The other day, she'd confessed to him that she wanted to be a director and a producer someday. He hadn't given her a strange look or questioned why. He'd just asked her how and when she planned to make it happen.

Tristan believed in the ambitions for her future as easily as he believed he could teach her how to ride a horse. Suddenly, the truth hit her where there was already a hollow, dull ache growing in her chest. Her heart. She wasn't falling for Tristan. She'd already fallen for him.

When she reached him, he took her into a loose embrace. "Did you finish packing?"

"Yes."

"How'd you sleep?" He looked more tired than usual.

"About as well as you."

"Then I feel sorry for you." He tightened his arms around her. "I tossed and turned all night. I missed having you with me."

"I missed you, too." His soft morning kiss had her lifting up on her toes as warmth uncoiled and expanded through her middle.

Tristan slowly ended the kiss. "Let's go for a ride."

A short time later, she rode Moonlight and he rode Thunder down one of the riding trails she hadn't been on. It wound through the trees along the edge of the south pasture.

After her first lesson at Tristan's house, Adam and Blake had taken over alternating as her riding instructors. As each day passed, and she'd started to doubt herself less, and trust her instincts more, as Tristan had suggested, she'd started to feel comfortable and secure in the saddle. And at her audition, if for some reason she fell off, well, she'd get up and get back on the horse. If the producers and Nash didn't choose her, she'd walk away knowing without a doubt that her own fears and judgments about herself didn't prevent her from getting the part.

As the trail narrowed, Tristan and Thunder fell behind her and Moonlight.

She glanced briefly over her shoulder. "Are you sure you want me leading the way? I don't know where we're going."

"Yes. We're just going a little ways up, and Thunder really likes the view in front of him."

Someone liked the view and it definitely wasn't Thunder. She laughed. "I bet he does."

Up ahead an area was chained off with a no-trespassing sign.

They halted in front of it and dismounted. Tristan unchained the sign, and they continued leading the horses down the path to a hitching post where they secured Thunder and Moonlight.

Tristan unbuckled a blanket from the rear of the saddle. He tucked it under his arm, then took her hand.

They walked a few yards ahead to a grassy clearing overlooking Tillbridge. He unfolded the blanket, and she helped him spread it under the tree. When they sat down, she scooted between his legs and he embraced her from behind.

As the sun rose higher, a long shadow moved from

left to right, revealing the expanse of green pasture below.

It took her breath away.

He kissed and nuzzled her neck. "This is my favorite spot."

"I can see why." She laid her hands over his and leaned in to him. "It's beautiful."

"Very beautiful." The quiet tone of his voice made her turn her face to look at him.

He traced his finger down her cheek. The way he looked at her made soft emotions swell in her chest and tears to prick in her eyes. She didn't want to spend her last few hours with him crying.

She faced away from him and looked out at the pasture, blinking tears away. "You told me that you wanted to expand Tillbridge. Tell me about it."

"You honestly want to hear about that?"

"I do."

He wrapped his arms around her and laid his cheek next to hers. "Well, with the stable, we can extend it out and add on more stalls…"

As he talked, she envisioned what he described in her mind. A future with his plans fully realized. But then the image transformed into more. Of her not just witnessing his dreams, but living them…with Tristan.

Chapter Twenty-Eight

"Cut!" Holland Ainsley called out from where she stood in the open field at a movie ranch outside of Los Angeles, gripping a medium-sized handheld digital cinema camera.

The former model turned director/producer was the epitome of sleek, on every level, from her hair gathered in an afro puff at the top of her head to the large round sunglasses perched on her light brown freckled nose, the white long-sleeved cropped sweater she wore, despite the heat, to the military-inspired camouflage pants tied at her ankles above her brown combat boots.

Nash Moreland looked equally cool and confident sitting on a black horse in front of the camera. For the Saturday late-morning audition, he'd completely embraced the character he'd play in *Shadow Valley*, wearing a tan cowboy hat, gray shirt, jeans and boots.

"Whoa." Chloe held on to the reins and naturally shifted her weight as Peanut, the chestnut-colored horse she was on, shuffled a bit to the left after he came to a stop. She'd managed to keep her cool on the horse, but compared to Holland and Nash, she felt like a wilted "before photo" in a makeover ad. Her pink button-down clung to her back, her thighs prickled underneath her jeans from the heat, and as much as she'd come to love her cowboy boots, she couldn't wait to slip on her favorite red flip-flops.

For the past two hours she'd been riding Peanut and interacting with him, Nash and Nash's horse in front of the camera. So far she'd managed to stay in the saddle while saying the lines she'd memorized from the new script she'd been sent yesterday. But had she embodied the character in a way that would lead Holland and Nash to choose her for the part?

The shot Holland had just filmed was about seeing if Chloe and Nash had that attention-getting chemistry that would captivate an audience and make their relationship believable on a movie screen.

Nash and Holland were in total sync about what they wanted for the movie. They'd already reached the point where they were adding onto or finishing each other's sentences.

"That was great." Holland grinned.

"I think we got everything we needed," Nash added.

Holland nodded. "I think we're done."

Nash got off his horse, handed the reins to the horse

trainer, and walked over to Holland who packed up her camera.

As Chloe dismounted, she released a long breath. Her audition was over. "Thanks for the ride, Peanut." She rubbed and stroked the horse near his neck and shoulder and he softly nickered.

Nash drifted over to the trainer loading the horses into a trailer.

Holland walked to Chloe carrying her camera bag. "Thanks for doing this. You did well. You looked like a natural on that horse."

Chloe shook her hand, fighting the urge to go into fangirl mode. "Thank you for giving me the opportunity to audition."

"I'm glad it worked that we could get you here on such short notice. Well, we'll be in touch as soon as we make our decision. Bye." Smiling, Holland gave a quick wave as she hurried off to her next meeting.

"She's right." Nash strolled over to Chloe.

Until a few hours ago, it had been years since she'd seen him, except for on a movie screen. For the most part, he looked the same. His hair was a deeper shade of blond. His smile revealed perfect capped teeth and more perfect cheekbones, and he sported a deep tan that he was trying on for the part he was playing in *Shadow Valley.*

He'd look fantastic on film as Montgomery the futuristic gunslinger with telepathic abilities and superhuman strength. But he had none of the grounded authenticity that Tristan naturally had.

He flashed a smile and peered at her from under the

brim of his hat. "You really did look like you belonged on a horse. Your time at Tillbridge Stable really paid off. I heard it's a really nice place. Lots of spectacular views."

Spectacular views? How did he know that? Maybe Lena had mentioned it to Holland and she'd told him. "Yes, it's a great place."

"There's a restaurant not far from here that makes killer fish tacos. I was planning to stop there for lunch. Join me? I'd love to catch up."

Honestly, going home and taking a shower sounded better, and she'd promised to call Tristan to tell him how she'd done. But this was probably also part of the audition, another chemistry test. Even though they were professionals and could act as if they liked each other, Nash getting along in real life with whoever scored the part would make things easier for everyone. And it would be nice to catch up.

Flipping the internal on switch that amped up her energy, she smiled. "Fish tacos sound fantastic. Let's do it."

Twenty minutes or so later, they walked into an establishment that had a café-like flair. Its vibrant decor of rich oranges, pinks and yellows made her think of Brewed Haven. Rina also had a thing for rich uplifting colors and a casual aesthetic.

They sat down in a corner booth with orange seats away from the other diners in the half-full space.

After they both ordered the tacos he'd mentioned, Nash leaned forward a bit in the seat opposite from her at the table. "I'm really looking forward to working with Holland. Her last films have been amazing. I'm sure you've seen them."

"Yes. No pun intended but the 'snowmageddon movie' completely blew me away. The visuals, and the actors' performances were spot-on. I just love her work. I really hope someday when I'm a director, I can do the same."

Nash's brow rose. "You're interested in directing?"

Now that she'd said it she couldn't take it back. And she didn't want to. "Yes. I want to direct."

"Have you mentioned that to Holland?"

"No. I figured the only thing I should be discussing with her right now is the part for this movie. And doing what I can to get this character right."

"I hear you." His expression grew sincere. "Like Montgomery—I'm still working out how to play him. He's hardworking, loyal and tough-minded."

Chloe sipped water from her glass. The character sounded a lot like Tristan. "That's definitely how I see him from what I read in the script."

"Yeah, but how do I lift him off the pages and make him real. What's grounding him to the cause?"

"Abandonment." The response came out without a thought.

Nash's brows narrowed in interest. "How? When?"

"Like what if one of his parents abandoned him. Wouldn't that bind him in some way to the other?"

"And that's driving his protective instincts." Nash leaned in farther. "Go on."

A few hours later, Chloe walked into her one-bedroom apartment, tired but exhilarated. She dropped her purse on the emerald couch.

The pothos plant in a purple pot on the dark wood coffee table, that the actors who'd stayed in her apartment had left her as a thank-you gift, thrived from the light shining through the side window.

Leary of inflicting her lack of plant mothering skills on the healthy, green vine-like plant with heart-shaped leaves, she'd planned to hand it over to Lena next time she saw her. Hopefully in a few weeks to sign her contract with the production company for the film.

Her audition really had gone well. And she had Tristan to thank for that. She found her phone in her purse and dialed his number. Her breathing shallowed a little in anticipation of hearing his voice.

Tristan answered. "Hey, I was just thinking about you."

A smile took over. "You were, huh?" He probably hadn't been thinking of her exactly but just wondering whether or not she'd done well for her audition.

"How did it go?"

"I stayed in the saddle." She walked past the high beige granite-topped counter separating the living room from the small kitchen on the right.

"I knew you would."

What sounded like a car door shutting along with passing cars came through on his end. She could also hear what were probably his footfalls connecting with concrete.

As Chloe grabbed the clear pitcher of water infused with lemons from the fridge, she envisioned where he might be in her mind as she filled the glass she'd

taken from a top cabinet. The parking lot at Tillbridge?
Downtown Bolan maybe? "I miss you."

"I miss you, too."

The rumble of his voice settled inside of her like
it always did, raising awareness and something else.
A calming sense of protection like when she was in
his arms.

"You know what I wish I could do with you right
now?" he asked.

"No. Tell me."

"Hold you."

"What else?"

His chuckle was low and sexy. "A lot more."

As her mind took over conjuring up what more
might look like, Chloe took another sip from her glass,
soothing her suddenly parched throat. But the coolness
of the water failed to quell the delicious warmth curl-
ing through her like wisps of smoke.

She released a shaky breath. "I like the sound of
that Too bad you can't send it to me special delivery."

"Maybe I can."

Chapter Twenty-Nine

Tristan rang the doorbell to Chloe's apartment. His grip involuntarily tightened on the handle of his large duffle as his heart beat a hair faster with each passing second. Had he made a mistake? Was she standing on the other side of the door right now trying to figure out what to do because she didn't want him there?

Chloe opened the door. "Tristan!"

She launched herself at him, and he barely had time to brace for her impact as she wrapped her arms around his neck and her legs around his waist.

As she kissed him on the lips, a smile he couldn't contain curled up his mouth as he wrapped his free arm around Chloe and carried her and his bag across the threshold.

"You're really here." She laid her cheek to his and

tightened her arms around him, making it a challenging balancing act as he dropped his duffle and shut the door.

Both hands free, he cupped her bottom with his hands and went in for what he'd been thinking about for days. A long lingering kiss. Was he imagining things or did she taste like lemons?

When they came up for air, she leaned back a little and looked into his eyes. "What are you doing here?" she asked softly.

"Like I told you over the phone a minute ago, I missed you."

There was more to it, but he wasn't ready to put the rest of what he felt into words. Tristan kissed her softly. Too many long hours had passed since she'd left. All he could think about was holding her. The cottage, hell the whole damn property had seemed empty without her voice, her smiles, her laughter.

Yesterday, he couldn't deal with it anymore. He'd informed Gloria, Blake and Philippa he was leaving, put them in charge, paid the exorbitant cost of the plane ticket for the short, last-minute trip, and got himself there.

One long soft kiss turned into another filled with fierce need that sparked fire in his veins. He reluctantly took his mouth from hers. "We should stop now."

"Why?" Her whispered response near his ear raised goose bumps over him.

Her barely there kisses trailing downward past the collar of his white button-down and her teeth nipping the side of his neck pulled a groan out of him. His growing erection pressed against the front of his jeans.

Tristan tightened his grasp on her butt. "I need you."

She kissed his earlobe. "The bedroom is straight down the hall."

No need to tell him twice. He heard her loud and clear.

A short time later, she lay under him on the pale peach sheets. The small amount of light let in through the closed blinds bathed her skin with a soft appealing glow. He soaked it in with slow kisses and caresses. The play of passion on her face as he glided his hand down her belly and lower still mesmerized him as she arched up to meet his touch.

Soon after, he glided inside of her, wound tight with need, unable to get enough of her softness and heat. On some level it scared him. On another it eased his mind and body more easily than any eight-second ride ever had for him.

He'd faced too many wrongs in his life to count, but Chloe wrapped around him in every way, including his heart, felt more than just right.

Coffee…it had to be there someplace. Tristan opened the top dark wood cabinets in Chloe's beige tiled-floor kitchen. A long narrow cabinet caught his eye in the corner. He opened it. *Jackpot.*

When he got up an hour ago this morning, one thing had been on his mind. Well two things. Kissing Chloe and making her breakfast. But she'd looked so sweet and peaceful, he couldn't bring himself to wake her up.

Between her audition and his unexpected arrival yesterday, she had to be tired. Instead he'd quietly cleaned up, dressed in a black T-shirt and navy blue sweats and closed the door to the bedroom as he'd left.

After hunting down mugs and figuring out the coffee maker on the counter, he moved to the next project on his list. Eggs. Maybe an omelet if he could find the right ingredients in her refrigerator.

She had most of the standard stuff he did, but he did find one unexpected food in her cabinet. Fruit Loops. That was one of his favorite cereals growing up. She never failed to surprise him. And why couldn't he stop grinning about that?

He'd just assembled the ingredients for a fresh basil, tomato and cheese omelet when he heard her in the bathroom. She could enjoy the coffee while he cooked. But he forgot something. What was it? Sugar for her coffee.

Tristan rummaged around and found it. The bedroom door opened and he poured the steaming coffee into a mug, then stirred in two teaspoons of sugar, just the way she liked it.

"Good morning." Chloe walked into the kitchen. She looked cute and comfortable in a pair of beige shorts and a white cropped tee. As she lifted on her toes and kissed him, he wrapped an arm around her waist. "What are we doing?" she asked.

With her lush curves pressed against him, his mind short-circuited for a moment. He reached for the cup of coffee he'd prepared for Chloe and handed it to her. "You're having coffee while I make breakfast."

"Okay." Smiling, she kissed him on the mouth, then drank from her the mug. "What are we having?"

"Omelets. Is there anything else you want with it?"

"We cou—"

A Drake ringtone sounded from her phone on the coffee table.

"That's Lena." Chloe plunked her mug down on the counter and rushed to answer her phone. "Hey. No, I'm up." She came back to the kitchen. "No I haven't heard anything. Uh-huh."

Tristan put a skillet on the stove. Lena was probably calling about her audition. Was "uh-huh" in response to something good or bad?

Chloe's shriek and jumping up and down in place filled in the blank. "This is the best news ever!" Smiling, she ran over to him and smacked her lips to his cheek. Just as he went to wrap an arm around her, she slipped away. "Hold on, Lena. Someone else is calling." She briefly checked the screen on her phone. "It's Nash. Yes, he has my number. I gave it to him yesterday when we had lunch. Hold on a sec. Hi, Nash. Yes, I just got the good news…"

Chloe had lunch with Nash Moreland *and* the dude had her number. Tristan worked to wrap his mind around that information as he cracked and whipped up the eggs. Well, he'd just have to get used to actors he watched in some of his favorite action movies having his girlfriend's phone number.

Girlfriend. That was one of the things he'd plan to establish before he left, possibly over breakfast. But now wasn't the time. Maybe at dinner that night? He was leaving in the morning.

Tristan glanced at Chloe who'd left the kitchen to pace the living room while talking on the phone to Nash. As he chopped up omelet ingredients, happiness for her good news intermingled with the nervousness of asking her to be his girlfriend. There were definitely reasons not to try a long-distance relationship, but he'd come up with just as many reasons for them to give it a shot on the flight from Maryland.

He and Chloe talked to each other so easily. They could continue to do that over the phone or Skype each other. If she was willing to fly out and see him when her schedule was free, he was more than ready to fly out and see her on weekends and longer when he could fit it in.

Chloe ended the call and came back to him. She was beaming with happiness. "I did it."

He hugged her. "Just like I knew you would."

She eased back and looked up at him with her soft brown eyes. "Thank you for all you did to help me."

Her phone chimed with a call. "It's Nash again."

He let her go so she could answer it and went back to making the omelet.

"Hey." She smiled as she listened. "A party... tonight." Her smile dimmed just a fraction. "I have a friend in town. He's only here for the weekend."

Friend. The word as it referred to him needled Tristan just a bit as he poured the eggs he'd beaten into the now hot skillet.

"Bring him to the party? I don't know." She looked

to Tristan, brow rising with a shrug as she posed the silent question.

She wouldn't ask him if she didn't want him to go and he'd spotted the look on her face. She wanted to attend the party.

"Sure." He added the basil, tomato and cheese to the eggs in the skillet.

"We'll be there," she said to Nash. "Okay. See you then." Chloe ended the call. She hugged Tristan from behind. "Are you sure you don't mind going to the party with me?"

He flipped the omelet closed. "It's related to the film. You should be there. I'm honored to go."

She kissed him on his nape. "It starts at eight. That gives us lots of hours to be together beforehand, and we won't stay late. Hey, do you have anything to wear tonight?"

Chapter Thirty

Fingers intertwined with each other's, Tristan ascended the stairs with Chloe to the upstairs living room in Nash's home.

Nash's place was just as large or not larger than the guesthouse at Tillbridge. From what Chloe had told him, Nash was single. What did he do with all the space?

More questions filtered into Tristan's mind. He was single, too, and the house he'd built suited him just fine, but was this the type of place she was striving to own in the future?

He glanced at Chloe. She'd chosen the same burgundy halter dress for the party that she'd worn the night they'd tried to share an intimate dinner at the Montecito. It showed off her smooth shoulders and toned bare legs. Instead of the ponytail she'd usually worn at Tillbridge, she'd straightened and curled her hair. Makeup made her skin appear even more flawless, and the red lipstick she had on made her lips look pouty and kissable. She was nothing short of stunning.

Good thing they'd gone shopping for him that afternoon. The distressed black jeans and lightweight black ribbed long-sleeved sweater she'd chosen for him fit with her. He'd wear the clothes again, and he'd probably even put on the black high-tops, every now and then, that she'd talked him into buying.

They walked through the upstairs arched entryway into the living room. A small party? There were at least sixty people, some of whom sat on the large black sectional in the middle while others mingled around the buffet tables against the side walls and the four bars positioned in the corners. On the far side of the room, a wall of glass gave a view of the clear night sky.

Chloe moved in front of him, leading the way as they slipped past people. Partway through the room, a blonde woman called her name. She let go of him to exchange hugs and air kisses with her.

As they moved through the crowd again, it became impractical to keep holding her hand as more people greeted her. She tried to pull him in for introductions, but no one seemed to be able to hear his name correctly above the noise in the room. By the time they reached the seating area, he'd been called Dustin, Justin, and Pete while others just ignored him.

Chloe squeezed his hand as she pressed herself

against his arm and leaned toward his ear. She had a worried expression. "You okay?"

For her, he would be. Tristan looked at her and smiled. "I'm fine." He pointed to the corner bar ahead to the left. "Do you want something to drink?"

"White wine would be nice."

"I'll get it. You mingle." Tristan went to the bar. He got a bottled beer for him, a microbrew he'd heard of but never tried, and the wine for Chloe.

But when he turned from the bar, he'd lost her in the crowd that had grown even larger.

He searched for her for a few minutes, but didn't see her.

People walked in and out of the sliding door on the glass wall.

Had Chloe gone outside? Tristan edged his way through the crowd. He looked left and spotted her talking to a group of people farther down the wide, lighted balcony overlooking a pool below.

When she saw him, she smiled and waved before being pulled back into the conversation.

Just as he took a step in her direction, someone clapped him on the back. Tristan turned.

It was Nash Moreland. In his action films, he'd seemed taller than Tristan, not shorter.

Nash smiled broadly. His teeth were almost the same color as his white button-down shirt. "Hey. How you doing? You must be Chloe's friend." Holding his own bottled beer, he went to shake Tristan's hand but noticed the drinks. He clapped Tristan on the back again instead. "Glad you could come."

"Anything to support Chloe. She worked hard to get here."

"Yeah, she's great and she's talented. We all wanted her for the part of Jessica in *Shadow Valley*." Nash tucked his hand casually into the front pocket of his jeans. As he drank his beer, he rocked back slightly in his brown suede-looking sneakers. From the looks of them, they were Converse All Stars. "And you're right about her working hard. She went to this place in Maryland to learn about horses and came back a natural with all this insight. This afternoon over lunch, we were talking about the character I'm going to play. It's the lead. I don't know if you know that I'm playing the lead?"

"She mentioned it." Tristan drank his beer and tamped down judgment about the look of self-importance on Nash's face. Yeah the guy was trying to impress him.

"Well, she gave me this fantastic backstory for my character Montgomery. Dad was a rodeo star. Hooked up with a woman. She got pregnant. Pops didn't know. Mom abandons the baby on his doorstep." Nash tapped his temple. "That's brilliant."

Seconds caught in the spin of disbelief, shutting out the rest of Nash's words. Chloe had fed his life story to Nash—something he'd never discussed with anyone outside his family—as a plotline over lunch?

Tristan glanced to where Chloe had been, but she was gone. Nash moved on, too.

Needing a minute to process his thoughts, Tristan walked to the railing and looked down at the pool where he saw Chloe standing with a group of people by the lighted pool.

She was laughing, carefree and drinking a white wine somebody had gotten her or that she'd gotten for herself from the bar tucked nearby.

Nash joined her group.

Disappointment still pinged in Tristan's gut over Chloe telling the story of him and his parents to Nash.

Someone tapped him on the shoulder. "Excuse me."

He looked to the petite redhead beside him. She flipped her hair over the emerald strap on her pale shoulder. "Are you one of the actors who's going to be in the film?"

"No." He gave her a polite smile. "I'm not an actor."

"Oh." She looked him up and down as if sizing him up. "So are you one of the producers or someone in charge of making the movie?"

"No."

"An athlete then?" She mentioned it as if it was a last resort to a potentially unsalvageable situation.

He shook his head, and she promptly dismissed him and walked away.

Chloe's laugh drifted up to Tristan.

Would she see him in the same way someday as the redhead who'd just approached him? That he wasn't important enough? Or maybe she already did. She hadn't valued that he'd entrusted her with the story about his parents. She should have at least called or texted him to see if it was okay to share it.

Down below, something was said that made the group laugh again. When Nash wrapped an arm around

Chloe's shoulders and gave her a squeeze, she didn't move away from him.

Acceptance and sadness settled inside of Tristan. In his mind's eye, he zoomed ahead, trying to see them together. What he saw was her growing tired of being with him. Just like at this party, she'd gravitate away from him to where she was happiest. To where she truly belonged.

Chapter Thirty-One

Chloe awoke to the sound of a zipper closing. She blinked, trying to clear the fog of sleep from her eyes.

Tristan's just-showered scent surrounded her.

She sat up peering across the room illuminated by the light from the adjoining bathroom.

Tristan, already dressed in a gray shirt and jeans, stood with his back to her, packing his bag that sat in her favorite red chair in the corner of the bedroom.

He had to leave for the airport at six to make his flight. Panic hit like cold water in the face. She snatched her phone from the nightstand. It was five forty. She released an inner groan. She'd meant to wake up with him at a quarter to four, maybe share a cup of coffee before he left, and talk.

She had screwed up on time last night, too. She'd

lost track of it and they didn't arrive home until after midnight.

On the way back to the apartment, she'd questioned Tristan about why he hadn't found her and made her aware of how late it was, and he'd said he hadn't wanted to get in her way.

"Hey." She pushed out the raspy whisper as she threw back the covers and got up. "Why didn't you wake me?"

"I didn't want to disturb you. I'm the one that has to leave, not you."

The same tone of quiet resignation that had been in his voice last night after the party remained. She'd asked him if something was wrong, and he'd said he was just tired.

She hurried into the bathroom and took care of the necessities.

When she came back out, the closed bag was on the floor, and he sat in the chair tying the laces on his black boots.

She rested her hand on his back. "How much time do we have until your ride share gets here?"

"About fifteen minutes. You really didn't have to get up."

He stood, and she wrapped her arms around his waist. "But I wanted to. You're leaving." The reality of that along with the unknown entity that had followed them home from the party drove her to rest her cheek to his chest, trying to get closer to him. "Tristan, please tell me what's wrong and don't tell me that it's nothing. You showed up happy and now you're not."

As he stroked her back, the heat of his palm penetrated her sleep shirt. His chest rose and fell under her cheek with a deep breath. "We don't have time to talk about it."

"Make time." Frustration made her release him and step back. "What's wrong? Just tell me."

"Did you tell Nash about my parents?"

Nash had mentioned meeting her friend when they were by the pool at his house last night. Puzzle pieces fell in place. Nash had told Tristan about their conversation over lunch about developing the backstory for Montgomery.

"Yes." His direct gaze made her fidget in place. She tugged at her sleep shirt. "But I didn't tell him it was you."

"You shouldn't have told him at all. Damn it, Chloe. My past isn't some make-believe scenario for someone to act out like they understand it. It's my life. It's real to me and I told you because I thought what we shared together was real. But I guess in this world that you live in, you can't tell the difference between a script and reality."

Echoes of what he'd said to her when they first met about acting and reality reared up, creating a nasty cocktail of guilt mixed in with more frustration. "I'm sorry, but you're not being fair. Yes, I should have thought it through, but it wasn't like that. I just got caught up in the excitement of the project. We all want this film to do well."

"And I completely understand." He bent down and picked up his bag. "Nothing mattered to you but getting the part in the movie, and now that you have it, nothing matters but the movie and whatever else it leads to in your career. You've made your priorities clear. There's no need to drag out what should have ended when you left Tillbridge."

One long flight later, Tristan walked into the guesthouse. As surly as he felt, he still greeted the receptionist and smiled at guests as he walked past the desk through a small sitting area with navy sectionals sitting in front of a built-in electric fireplace in the wall.

Through the open restaurant doors in front of him, guests and local customers filled the restaurant for breakfast.

He turned right and walked down the corridor with restrooms and a gold-tiered literature stand filled with brochures of places and activities in the local area. At the end, he knocked on the plain wood door.

"Come in." Zurie called out behind it.

She sat at an oak desk in the well-cared-for brown leather chair that had been her father's tapping on her computer keyboard, absorbed in something on the wide-screen computer.

An inbox sat on one top corner and an out-box on the other. The wide-screen computer and one short neat stack of files were the only other items. A filing cabinet sat tucked in the corner behind her next to a tall green plant. On the opposite side of the office sat a small round meeting table with navy padded chairs, matching the two sitting in front of her desk.

What the neat, efficient-looking, modern space

lacked in decor, the windows with a view of cut lawn and trees lining the property made up for it.

A few hours ago, when he'd landed in Baltimore from California, several texts and voice mails from Philippa and Gloria had been on his phone telling him that Zurie had come home.

One voice mail had been from Zurie, telling him she wanted to see him at seven that morning.

"Hey." She glanced at him briefly and gestured to the chairs in front of her desk. "Take a seat. I'll be with you in a minute. I just need to finish reviewing this letter Jess typed up."

Her virtual assistant, Jess, lived on the West Coast. Despite the time difference and the distance, the two had made it work. Jess had been with her for years.

He set his phone on the edge of her desk and took a seat in one of the chairs.

A minute or so later she turned her attention to him. "How was your trip?" Zurie leaned back in the chair.

Tristan settled more into his. "Productive."

She raised a brow. "And last minute."

"Seems to be the trend around here."

Her eyes narrowed a bit as she studied him. "Business reasons are one thing. Personal are another. You seem to lean toward the latter."

Still recovering from what happened with Chloe and a sleepless night, he wasn't in the mood to spar or explain himself. Tristan went all in. "Stop poking around whatever you want to say to me and just say it."

"All right, if that's the way you want it. I'm supposed to sign papers next week giving you ownership in the stable." As she sat back in the chair, she lifted her hands in a partial shrug. "You running off twice since I left you in charge raises concern."

"About?"

"What these past two years were all about. Exploring your commitment to the stable."

Exploring? That's what she was calling it now? "No." He sat back ready to dig in. "That's not what me working with you has been about. It was a loyalty test and I passed. I've given you and Tillbridge nothing but my commitment for the past two years. You calling me going away twice, for a few days, while delegating tasks to more than capable people is a problem with you, not me."

Zurie expression cooled to all business as she leaned forward. "And that's where you've always been short-sighted about all of this. You see a loyalty test or me questioning your capabilities. I see you doing the same things you did before you left: avoiding calls, reconnecting with your bull riding buddies, running off to do who knows what and why." She stabbed her finger into the top of the desk as her voice raised. "I don't have time to figure you out. The job of running this place is bigger than you and me. It's about protecting Tillbridge…and the people here that you should care about."

Should care about? Just as he was about to go on the defensive, in a rare moment of vulnerability, he caught a glimpse of a younger Zurie. The one he'd had to leave to protect. Emotional pain beyond guilt pierced into him as he hurt for that version of her. She'd weathered storms, just like he had, doing what she just said, protecting Tillbridge when he couldn't. He'd done a lot of things trying to make up for it…except one.

The words born from his sudden realization came out on their own. "I'm sorry I wasn't here for you."

She reared back a little. "What?" Her face a mix of confusion and doubt, probably about if she'd heard him right or even if the apology he should have given her years ago was sincere.

"I wasn't here after your father died, and because of that, you had to make sacrifices on your own to keep Tillbridge going. It shouldn't have been that way."

For a second, it looked as if the wall she'd let slip was going back up. "Why did you just leave?"

Why? To him it was a hard question. For her, it was about him having kept her in the dark without an explanation. He saw it then in her eyes. They'd been close once, and he'd hurt her the most by shutting her out.

His phone drew his gaze. He'd viewed the recording Chloe had made of Erica at the cottage as a way of absolving him from blame, and he hadn't seen the point of doing that. He'd believed they just needed to move on and forget about the past, but Zurie needed answers before she could move on to anything with him.

Tristan reached forward, picked up his phone, and accessed the recording. "I'll let Erica answer that question. I need you to listen to something."

"Erica? What does she have to do with this?"

"Just listen. You'll understand." He hit Play and set the phone back on her desk. For most of it, the voices were too low to make out, except for one critical part.

Just hearing Erica's voice irritated him. He stood and paced away from the desk as the recording played. It finally reached the crucial moment.

"There were wealthier men out there. Why marry him?"

"I didn't have a choice. Don't you dare stand there and judge me. I was broke, and in debt and I had nowhere else to go. He gave me a way out, and I took it. Maybe I wouldn't have if you would have been here instead."

Incredulity filled Zurie's face. "That's Erica…when was this recorded?"

"Around two weeks ago." He stopped the recording and picked up his phone.

Her mouth remained agape for a moment, then she pointed at the phone in his hand. "So if I'm reading between the lines correctly, she wanted you instead of your father. I know you wouldn't do anything, but did she try anything like…" She grimaced with a look of distaste as if trying to find the words but not liking any of the available ones. "Try to hook up with you?"

"Two days before I left."

"Did you tell Uncle Jacob?"

"I didn't get a chance." Tristan told her what happened from beginning to end, including his father's ultimatum.

Zurie closed her eyes a moment and shook her head. "But why didn't you tell me or Rina what happened? Maybe we could have done something."

"And make you two choose between them or me? I was afraid that if Dad thought I was stirring the pot with you two against them, he'd make good on his threat and distance himself. Besides that, Erica only let me see the truth about her. She showed everyone else the facade of a loving wife. All everyone talked about was how happy he was. And when it came to running Tillbridge, you needed him more than you needed me."

"No." She stood and walked over to him. "That's not true. How could you even think that?" Zurie gave him a small sad smile. "I'd envisioned us stepping up as the new generation, just like Dad and Uncle Jacob used to talk about when we were younger."

"I did, too." He laid his hand on her shoulder. "But you had the most experience running this place, I didn't and Dad had all of the connections. People that may not have done business with us if he would have walked away. And truthfully, I needed a minute. I was still adjusting after getting back from my last tour in the Middle East. Me staying wasn't worth the risk of me possibly ending up being dead weight to you in running this place."

Zurie stared at her feet. When she looked back up, her eyes were bright with unshed tears but a little more than a hint of irritation showed on her face. "I understand why you did what you did, but I don't agree with it."

She glared at him but there was also a softness in her expression. Something he hadn't witnessed in forever on her face when she'd looked at him. Seeing that small concession in her gave him hope. "Does this mean we can call a truce, sign the papers and move forward as partners?" He extended his hand to her.

"A handshake?" She batted it away and wrapped her arms around him. "For the record, I'm still mad at you."

Tentative, and rusty from lack of use, their embrace paled in comparison to their bear hugs of the past, but it was a start.

She released him. "But I'm hella-pissed at Erica. Earlier this year, I found an inventory of Uncle Jacob's collection in a file. You know how he hated paperwork. Who knows how it got there. Anyway, now we can inventory what she sent over and make sure everything is there. And if it's not, we not only have the inventory, but her words, proving that she's shady. I'm so glad you made the recording."

"I didn't. Chloe did. She was in the other room when Erica showed up. She wasn't able to get everything, but she got the parts that mattered."

The part that had just allowed him to begin to make amends with Zurie so they could close that chapter of their pasts and focus on building a new one.

"Well, make sure you tell her thank you for me," Zurie said.

The sinking feeling that he'd battled whenever he thought of her, since leaving LA, took all the air from his lungs. He forced a breath. "We're not together anymore. I care about her, but we're on different paths. She's committed to her career. I'm committed to Tillbridge. I won't be seeing her again."

Zurie's expression sobered. "Well…now's probably a good time for me to tell you why I wanted to meet today." As she headed back to the desk chair, she pointed to the seat he'd vacated. "You should sit down…"

Chapter Thirty-Two

Tristan sat back in his desk chair, blinking away eye strain from staring at the computer reading through the inventory report. Gloria had sent it to him before leaving for the day a couple of hours ago.

He could see that she'd been puzzled that he'd asked for it so late. Friday nights, he usually knocked off early and headed to the Montecito, but the desire wasn't there. He would have just spent the night thinking about Chloe...and that she was coming back.

The production company for the movie that Chloe's auditioning for hit a snag with the owners of the horse farm where they were planning to film. Something involving contracts and money. Lena referred them to me about filming here at Tillbridge...

That's what Zurie had told him. Since then, it had

been a revolving door of people associated with the film production checking out the property. Even though they hadn't signed the ownership papers yet, Zurie had kept him in the loop with the negotiations. She'd done well. Not only would film company pay to use Tillbridge, but they'd build the indoor arena and a structure they could turn into an additional stable once the filming ended.

It was a win-win situation for them and the production company, but things were moving fast. He had to find a way to wrap his mind around seeing Chloe again…with Nash. In a month the cast, including Chloe, were staying at Tillbridge for an immersion experience of learning about horses and working at the stable.

A knock sounded on the side door in the hallway outside his office. The stable was locked up for the night. Only he was there.

Tristan switched to the video camera feed on his computer and clicked on the one over the outside door that opened into the hallway.

It was Mace. He wasn't in uniform. Turning, he looked directly at the camera. Of course he knew Tristan was watching him.

Tristan walked into the hall to unlock and open the door.

Mace strolled in carrying a plastic shopping bag. "Hey." He headed straight to the office giving Tristan no choice but to follow him.

He did after he relocked the door. As soon as Tristan sat behind his desk, Mace who sat on the other side of it, reached into his bag, pulled out two beers, and used the edge of the desk to pop the tops.

Tristan accepted the one he handed him. "Let me guess. Gloria called you."

"She did. Along with a few other people who reached out to me about you."

"Other people? Who?"

Mace chuckled, then drank from his beer. "You really are out of it if you don't know the answer to that question." He ticked off names on his fingers. "Try Philippa, Rina, and then there was Wes. Blake and Adam just ambushed me down at the Montecito tonight, and oh, Zurie."

"Zurie?" Tristan was baffled. "Why?"

"They claim you haven't been the same since you got back from your trip this past Monday. Honestly, I thought they were exaggerating, but you look like hell."

"Thanks a lot. And they sent you here to cheer me up." Tristan huffed a breath. "What were they thinking?"

"That you needed a friend. So from what I understand, you went to California to see Chloe. What happened? Last I heard things were going well between the two of you."

The sincerity in Mace's gaze made Tristan regret sniping at him. Maybe he did need to talk about it, and Mace was the one to talk to. The man was a vault. He wouldn't repeat what was said.

Tristan took a long pull from his beer. "Things were good while we were here, but in California, things were different."

"How so?"

"Do remember how she looked the first day she was here? Well, magnify that by five."

Mace's brow rose. "Maybe I shouldn't. She is your girlfriend."

"Was my girlfriend." A bitter chuckle escaped him. "Actually, we never made it to that stage. That's why I went there. To ask her."

"She said no. Damn." Mace shook his head. "That's tough."

"Yeah, it was tough, but not because she said no. I didn't ask her. I couldn't. Like I said she was different." Seeing that change was harder to accept than her telling Nash about his past. Sharing his story was possibly a slip, but how she'd looked and acted in LA, that was hard fact. Sipping his beer, he washed that realization down inside of him where it just sat, taking up too much space. "She was Chloe Daniels, the actress. Not the Chloe who was here. I belong here. She doesn't. She belongs in Hollywood, living that life. That's what's important to her. She'd never be happy here and ultimately that's what I would have wanted. Her, here at Tillbridge with me."

That was the first time he'd actually said it—that was what he wanted. For Chloe to call Tillbridge home someday.

Mace set his beer on the desk and settled back in the chair. "Did you tell her that?"

"No. Why would I when I know she doesn't want the same?"

"Because that's her choice to make not yours to assume." Mace pointed at him. "You wimped out and didn't ask her, so now you're sitting here feeling like you got kicked in the gut over a question you never got the answer to."

Tristan went to refute what he said…and couldn't. Yeah, he'd assumed. "But you didn't see her. It was like a glove she slipped right into."

"So she was in the zone, doing her thing."

"Exactly."

"Like you were in the zone while you were riding bulls or like I'm in the zone when I put on my uniform. That's her job. You should be able to relate to that and understand the shift in attention. But I'm confused. At first you said things were different in California but just now you said *she* was different. Are you saying the two of you being together didn't feel right anymore?"

Holding her. Making love to her. Just being around her. None of that was different.

He set his half-full beer on the desk, no longer interested in drinking it. "No. It was more than just right."

"If that's the case, why are you sitting here being miserable instead of finding a way to make things work with her?"

"What if she doesn't want the same things that I do?"

Mace looked him in the eyes. "What if she does and just because you won't talk to her you're missing out because you're too afraid to—"

"You don't have to say it." Tristan already knew what was coming. "Because I won't take the risk."

Take the risk. It was the same advice that Mace had

given him weeks ago when he was on the fence about getting involved with Chloe. It was also something that he already innately knew. But what if he was right and trying to pursue a relationship with her was a big mistake. But what if by not risking it all, he lost the chance of what he wanted with every part of him… forever with Chloe.

Chapter Thirty-Three

As Chloe trekked across the parking lot of the stable at Tillbridge, gravel crunched under her cowboy boots. Just as it had when she'd first arrived there two days ago, the familiarity of the place filled her with a mix of emotions.

Shivering, she tucked her hands into the short dark jacket, emblemized with the name of the film on the back and her name on the front left side.

The unusually cool morning, the result of some freak storm, was supposed to be replaced by summer-like temperatures later on. She'd peel off the layers once the sun rose, taking off the jacket and spending the rest of the day in just her T-shirt, jeans and boots.

If only she could shed the memories of Tristan as easily.

Him not being there during the two weeks of orientation at the stable with the cast of the movie before they started filming brought her a sense of relief and sadness. Gloria had told her that he and Adam were picking up rescue horses in Georgia and North Carolina. Still, she'd found herself looking for him, wishing she could see him so maybe they could talk. She wanted to apologize and for them to exist in the same space without him hating her. Her feeling like she couldn't breathe whenever she thought about him breaking things off, that would take some time.

Back in LA, she'd lain awake at night wondering how she could stay focused in a place that reminded her strongly of him. She'd given in to the idea that had persisted in her mind the most—returning to the last place he'd taken her before she'd left for her audition. He didn't want to talk to her so what she couldn't say to him would be shared with the trees and the horses in the pasture, instead of Tristan. But maybe just saying the words trapped in her heart might give her the closure as well as the strength she'd need to stay focused, especially once filming started.

At the far corner of the parking lot near an entrance to the trail, Blake waited for her with a golf cart.

She'd wanted to saddle up Moonlight for the ride and lose herself in the grooming of the horse afterward, but she didn't have time. Orientation at the stable with the rest of the cast was happening in a couple of hours. Actors who showed up late risked being labeled as prima donnas, expecting people to wait for them. That wasn't the impression she wanted to make.

She hugged Blake and returned his smile. "Thank you for signing this out for me. I won't be gone long."

He waived off her concern. "Take your time. You're family. Just park it back here when you're done and I'll take care of it."

"Thanks." *Family...* As Chloe got in and released the brake she had to avoid looking at him as she blinked back tears. As surreal as it was to be there, and not see Tristan, Tillbridge did feel like home.

She'd anticipated more awkward moments with the staff, coming back under the circumstances of their breakup, but to her relief, they'd greeted her with genuine smiles. Even Zurie had given her a big hug in the reception area at the guesthouse when she'd first arrived.

Everyone welcoming her back, along with the excitement buzzing through the stable and the guesthouse in anticipation of what was to come with filming the movie there—meeting the actors, the possibility of snagging parts as extras—had lifted some of her own weighty feelings.

As Chloe steered the golf cart down the straightaway, the sun rose higher. Soft white rays shone through the tree leaves creating prisms of light illuminating the trail. She slowed down over the dips and the final curve and parked at the bottom of the slight incline. After grabbing the blanket Blake had left for her on the passenger seat like she'd asked, Chloe hiked upward to the overlook above the pasture. Then she spread out the blanket and sat where Tristan had held her and told her about his dreams for Tillbridge.

The memory took shape of the way he'd looked at

her, the way he'd smiled as he'd talked, and how he'd taken breaks in between what he'd said just to kiss her.

Now, all the things he'd wanted were in his grasp, the expansion plan, ownership in Tillbridge. When she'd talked to Rina, she'd heard he'd even gotten his father's memorabilia back.

Chloe shut her eyes, still seeing Tristan's face on the day he'd told her about his ambitions for the stable. Remnants of the happiness she'd felt for him then intertwined with sadness that she couldn't help him celebrate now.

Bitter and sweet wrapped around her heart and squeezed. If she hadn't hurt him, she would have been.

My past isn't some make-believe scenario for someone to act out like they understand it. It's my life. It's real to me and I shared it with you because I thought what we had together was real. But I guess in this world that you live in, you can't tell the difference between a script and reality.

Remembering Tristan's last words to her in LA hit even harder now and she sucked in a breath.

He'd said she couldn't tell the difference between a script and reality. The funny thing was, a few days after he'd left, it had become clear to her just how much her norm had shifted completely. Los Angeles didn't feel real to her anymore. It was a place filled with people to know, places to be and opportunities to strive for, but they felt less tangible than the sun beaming down from a clear open sky, or the earthy scents of a just-mown pasture, an oiled leather saddle and the smell of fresh hay. She craved them along with the steady hoofbeats of horses over honking car horns in the midst of traffic-filled LA. Heck. She even missed Thunder Bay's orneriness.

Her phone buzzed in the pocket of her jacket with a sixty forty-five reminder alarm, alerting her that she was due at the stable by seven thirty. Chloe took it out, tapped the snooze button, then set it beside her. She still had a little more time.

She'd come there to apologize and find closure, right? Chloe lay on the blanket, closed her eyes and thought of Tristan from his close-cut dark hair to his booted feet.

The vision morphed to the day long ago when she'd ruined her favorite red boots and almost fallen on her butt. Tristan had been so irritated with her but in retrospect, having gotten to know him, he'd been tender in his own way when he'd moved her out of the path of the horses. He'd just wanted to keep her safe, and in that moment, she'd felt nothing less than protected by him.

More memories rolled in. Of them saving E.J., kissing in the rain, dancing at the Spring Fling, their magical trip to his home. Tristan getting her on a horse and reminding her to have faith in herself…and then LA.

She swallowed hard as sadness tightened her throat. "Tristan, I'm sorry. You shared your life with me and I broke your trust by not respecting what that meant. It was careless of me to do that and to not think how that would hurt you." Tears leaked from her eyes to her cheeks. "But you were wrong when it came to me winning the part. That wasn't the most important thing and neither is the success of the movie. You are. I'd rather be here with you, because…" She drew in a shaky breath to push out the rest. "I love you with all my heart."

A soft whinny coming from the short trail where she'd left the golf cart, instead of far away in the field, made her sit up and open her eyes.

Tristan stood a few feet away, his back toward her as he looked out at the pasture. He was dressed similarly to how he was on the day they'd met, but he wore his black Stetson.

With sun shining in front of him, he was like a spectacular, wonderful mirage. The perfect, sexy cowboy. Maybe she was dreaming. He'd rarely worn his hat around the stable when she'd been there.

"Tristan?"

He turned and faced Chloe.

Her heart tripped. He was really there. Why was he there? Was he pleased to see her? Of course he wasn't. This was his spot, and she was trespassing. Again.

She rose to her feet. "I was just leaving. I didn't mean to intrude. I thought you were gone." Chloe bent to retrieve her phone and the blanket, but her shaking hands made her clumsy and she failed.

Tristan lightly grasped her arm. "Chloe…we should talk."

"You don't have to say it." Chloe couldn't bring herself to look up from his chest. If she did she might cry even harder. "I understand completely. I won't get in your way while I'm here. I'm a professional. We both are. We can keep our personal feelings out of the situation."

"I don't think we can." Tristan tipped up her chin

with his finger and his intense hazel-brown gaze held hers. "Because I love you, and you love me, unless I'm hearing things."

Was *she* hearing things? Maybe he was actually telling her to go away, and she was making up her own story in her mind about what she wanted him to say.

Doubts started to dissolve as he curved his hands to her waist, leaned in, and pressed his lips to hers.

Chloe slid her hands up his chest and around his neck, falling deeper and deeper into a kiss that explored, laid claim and made her heart swell with relief and joy that he was there…he was really there.

They eased back from the kiss but held on to each other.

Her phone buzzed on the ground with another short reminder alarm. She needed to get back, but there was so much she wanted to say, no, needed to say to him right now.

Chloe lowered her hands to his chest. "You heard the I love you part right, but did you also hear that I was sorry for sharing your story? I never should have done that."

"I heard you and I forgive you." He kissed her palm and lowered their intertwined hands back to his chest. "But I should have stayed so we could have worked it out instead of leaving. Next time, I will."

"Next time." She couldn't stop a smile. "I like the sound of that."

A solemn expression came over his face. "I have to be honest. The main reason I left wasn't about what you told Nash. It was seeing you in your element with your friends. It made me wonder, if what I have to offer is enough for you."

It pained her to see uncertainty in his eyes. She cupped his cheek. "When I say I love you, I mean every part of you. I don't need anyone else and I don't want you to change. Acting is my job and I like doing it, but I love that I can just be myself with you."

"But your job is important to you, and I know you have ambitions for the future. I want to see you achieve all of that." A small smile came over his mouth. "And to hear you thank Thunder for helping you get there when you win an award. I also have to be here, taking care of Tillbridge, but I'm also all in to being with you. I'm willing to do the long-distance thing if you are."

The sincerity in his eyes, and knowing that he wanted to support her dreams as much as she supported his, brought happy tears to her eyes. "I'm all in, too. Planes, cars, trains, whatever it takes for us to cover the miles and make this work."

"What about horses?" As he tightened his arms around her, humor filled his expression.

As always, Tristan's strength, his smile and now the love she saw in his eyes, made her heart kick up a beat.

As she smiled back up at him, Chloe took off his Stetson and set it on her head. "Definitely horses."

* * * * *

*Don't miss Rina's book, next in
the Tillbridge Stables miniseries,*
Her Sweet Temptation

*Available October 2020 wherever
Harlequin Special Edition books
and ebooks are sold!*

COMING NEXT MONTH FROM

⊕ HARLEQUIN

SPECIAL EDITION

Available June 16, 2020

#2773 IN SEARCH OF THE LONG-LOST MAVERICK

Montana Mavericks: What Happened to Beatrix?
by Christine Rimmer

Melanie Driscoll has come to Bronco seeking only a fresh start; what she finds instead is Gabe Abernathy. The blond, blue-eyed cowboy is temptation enough. The secrets he could be guarding are a whole 'nother level of irresistible. Peeling the covers back on both might be too much for sweet Mel to handle...

#2774 A FAMILY FOR A WEEK

Dawson Family Ranch • by Melissa Senate

When Sadie's elderly grandmother mistakes Sadie and Axel Dawson for a happily engaged couple, they decide to keep up a week-long ruse. The handsome rugged ranger is now playing future daddy to her toddler son...and loving fiancé to her. Now if only she can convince Axel to open his guarded heart and join her family for real...

#2775 HIS PLAN FOR THE QUINTUPLETS

Lockharts Lost & Found • by Cathy Gillen Thacker

When Gabe Lockhart learns his friend Susannah Alexander wants to carry her late sister's frozen embryos, he can't find a way to support her. And his next Physicians Without Borders mission is waiting... But five years later, Gabe comes home to Texas to find Susannah is a single parent—of toddler quintuplets! Can he stay in one place long enough to fall for this big family?

#2776 A MOTHER'S SECRETS

The Parent Portal • by Tara Taylor Quinn

Since giving her son up for adoption, Christine Elliott has devoted herself to helping others have families of their own at her fertility clinic. But when Jamison Howe, a widowed former patient at the clinic, reenters her life, she finds herself wondering if she is truly happy with the choices she made and the life she has...or if she should take a chance and reach out for more.

#2777 BABY LESSONS

Lovestruck, Vermont • by Teri Wilson

Big-city journalist Madison Jules's only hope for an authentic parenting column rests with firefighter Jack Cole and his twin baby girls. But the babies unexpectedly tug on her heartstrings...as does their sexy dad. When opportunity knocks, Madison is unsure if she still loves the draw of the big city until she learns Jack isn't who she thought he was...

#2778 MORE THAN NEIGHBORS

Blackberry Bay • by Shannon Stacey

Cam Maguire is in Blackberry Bay to unravel a family secret. Meredith Price has moved next door with her daughter. He's unattached. She's a widowed single mom. He's owned by a cat. She's definitely team canine. All these neighbors have in common is a property line. One they cross...over and over. And Cam thought he knew what he wanted—until his family's secret changes everything.

HSECNM0620

Tears continuing to spill from her eyes, she pushed away
from him and let out a shuddering breath. Her chest rose
and fell with each agitated breath. "Just…everything."
She gestured helplessly.

"Are you worried about the kids?" Given what Mitzy
had showed her, she shouldn't be.

"No." Susannah took another halting breath, still
struggling to get her emotions under control. "You saw
them," she said, making no effort to hide her aggravation
with herself. "They were thrilled. They always are when
they get to spend time with the other dads."

"Which is something they don't have."

She pressed on the bridge of her nose. "Right." She swallowed and finally looked up at him again, remorse glimmering in her sea-blue eyes. "It just makes me feel guilty sometimes, because I know they're never going to have that."

He brought her back into the curve of his arm. "You don't know that," he said gruffly.

Taking the folded tissue he pressed into her hand, Susannah wiped her eyes and blew her nose. "I'm not saying guys wouldn't date me, if benefits were involved."

"Now you're really selling yourself short," he told her in a low, gravelly voice.

"But no one wants a ready-made family with five kids."

I would, Gabe thought, much to his surprise. "I'd take you all in a heartbeat," he said before he could stop himself.

Don't miss
His Plan for the Quintuplets *by Cathy Gillen Thacker,*
available July 2020 wherever
Harlequin Special Edition books and ebooks are sold.

Harlequin.com